MW01254455

five Past Twelve

by

Robert N. Shapiro

authorHOUSE®

AuthorHouse™
1663 Liberty Drive, Suite 200
Bloomington, IN 47403
www.authorhouse.com
Phone: 1-800-839-8640

First published by AuthorHouse 4/14/2008

ISBN: 978-1-4343-5242-2 (sc)

Library of Congress Control Number: 2007909913

Printed in the United States of America
Bloomington, Indiana

This book is printed on acid-free paper.

"In the Middle of Difficulty,
Lies Opportunity."

-Albert Einstein

Chapter 1

Everything had become so generic. I wonder if others had experienced this lack of sensation, or if they have become numb to it. I feel as if the only people who are different are the ones who try so hard to be. I find that I hate them as well. The same questions and responses are constantly thrown around: What's your favorite band, The Beatles, Dave Matthews or Britney Spears? Oh fuck not Nickelback. What's your favorite color? Is it blue? Oh, you're a Yankees fan and by the way, nice Che Guevara t-shirt. Every person is the same slave to the same trends, merely an advertisement with a circulatory system; hardly vibrant, conscious and breathing people.

I sat at the circular wooden table in the dimly lit bar feverishly tapping my right leg. I was beginning to feel the drug slide down my nasal cavity and coat my throat. I knew that within the next half an hour or so I would feel the draining effects of coming down. As well I instinctively knew that once that feeling set in, I would end the date and seek further means to get high. Earlier on, as soon as I began breaking up three slender white lines on a CD case in my dorm room, I knew that getting high before going on a blind date was completely idiotic. I deemed it to be a more attractive option than having to wait until the date was over. The stupidity lies in the fact that the high would last roughly forty to forty-five minutes, and it took about twenty minutes to arrive at the bar, therefore I was looking at roughly twenty minutes into the date before I would become twitchy and the craving would become insurmountable. The thought of breaking some up beforehand, placing it in a vial and bringing it along crossed my mind but I immediately discarded it. As soon as I arrived at my destination I regretted my decision.

I wasn't even sure why I was here. I should never have listened to Peter. He told me repeatedly that she was slutty, smart, and shy. Smart and shy I can go for, but why he went out of his way to mention she was slutty is odd. I know it's been awhile, but I am not the least bit bothered. I mean I was in a year long relationship, so what's the rush? Shit, is that her? Appearance fits the description. She's kind of pretty, well…prettier than me.

My train of drug inspired thoughts was suddenly interrupted by a soft and feminine voice.

"Are you Jack?" Lindsay said, ducking her head at the last moment to peer up out of her green eyes. The night before on the phone, I gave her a description of myself including what I was planning on wearing.

"You got it. You're Lindsay I take it?" I asked knowing the answer. We only get so many breaths in this lifetime I really wish that I didn't ask so many questions to which

I know the answer. I have to be more economical in my speech in the future. She sat down in the chair right next to me. For a brief second, I thought about getting up to shake her hand or maybe pulling out her chair, but they were just passing thoughts. I mean, any time an act of kindness is extended from a man to a woman (or visa versa) it is misconstrued as a sexual advance, so I am better off without even bothering.

She was extremely well kept, almost waspy in her demeanor, and, yes, I view this as a negative. She was average looking; her face had pointy features and was rather pale but not awful to look at by any means. She wouldn't catch my eye if she stood in any sort of crowd, yet at the same time I probably wouldn't kick her out of bed. I can only imagine what she was thinking about me. I always thought there was nothing special about the way I look at all. She is shorter than me as I stand at a rather uneventful 5'8", so I appreciate Peter's foresight into that aspect of my self-consciousness. Lindsay had shoulder-length, natural blonde hair, and ordinary but wide, dark brown eyes. She was neither thin nor fat nor curvy.

She finally broke the silence. I tend to think too much which leads to long periods of awkward silence. Word to the wise: avoid thinking on blind dates.

"So, Peter told me you're a marketing student?"

I had to think for a second. I have changed my major so many times I was drawing a blank. I guess Peter must have spoken to her about me prior to mid-August when I changed my major.

"No, actually I am a history student now," I replied, after what felt like a long delay. I wondered what she thought about that delay. It's like when someone asks you your age and you momentarily forget.

"Oh, so you changed your major from marketing to history." she said.

"Well, actually, I went from marketing to pre-law to sociology, and now I have finally settled on history." I knew my convoluted academic life would raise questions, all of which I would have loved to dodge.

She let out an exaggerated laugh, which I was sure she hadn't meant to direct at me. I didn't mind because I knew, once her laughter subsided, the barrage of questions would commence.

"So, tell me why the changes, Jack?"

People were so easy to predict. A spontaneous comment, question or answer in a conversation was as rare as a steroid-free homerun race. Alright, so here I go, attempting to explain myself… "I just realized how empty the corporate world is; staring at a computer for forty years of your life, crunching irrelevant numbers. I hate corporations and pencil-pushers; they are a collective and manipulative drain on society. I also hate advertisements and the people who saturate society with them." God, I've given this speech so many times.

She proceeded to interrupt my speech, "Easy tiger, I get it. I disagree with you, but sounds like you made the right call." She said with another one of her inane nervous laughs, which I found grating.

"Tell me, what do you study?" I knew the answer was going to be psychology or a four year degree in finding a husband. One day I really have to find the root of my misogyny, but for now it'll have to do.

"I study psychology"

Laughter filled my body, containing it was a hard-fought mission.

"Of course" I just can't be phony.

The bar we decided to meet at was probably one of the more popular ones on campus. It was called The Hound. It was nothing special, and could use a little more in the ambience department. It was the kind of place you went to when you couldn't get laid in a nice place. It was relatively close to my residence room, so it would have to do. I was getting fed up with the empty banter being thrown back and forth. I knew I was coming down from my high as my mouth was parched and nose was beginning to run slightly.

"Listen Lindsay, this has been alright but I think I am going to call it a night." I said hoping she wouldn't ask why, because I didn't have a reason that didn't make me sound like a complete loser.

"Oh ok, well this was quicker than I thought it would be. We've only been here fifteen minutes. Maybe we'll get together on the weekend and continue this." She said as she flashed a little awkward smile my way.

"Yeah we'll see. I have your phone number so I will give you a shout."

"Bye" she replied as I began walking away. Shit, should I have walked her back to her room? But then she would have thought I wanted to come in or something. Oh well, I was already outside, so no reason to act chivalrous now. Rest in peace chivalry, you had a great run.

It was a gorgeous night, and the campus was a ghost town, I guess students don't go out on Tuesdays. I walked past the student centre and thought about my first fifteen months living on my own. I always dreaded those rites of passage that everyone talked about, but no one ever noticed they were experiencing. My mom wept when I left. I knew it would be tough for her, but she has her new husband now. I proceeded up the cement stairs towards Drake Residence.

I stopped to grab one of the campus newspapers, the last one lying in a beat-up old newspaper stand. These papers were always informative about nonsense. The headline announced the forthcoming student elections. As I perused the candidates and their "political" platforms, I realized how they were all so similar including their ethnical background. What was the point? Whoever would be elected would just become an appendage of the administration, an administration that runs an educational institution as a corporation, as they line their own pockets. Campus elections were a microcosm of real politics, which disgusted me and numbed my insides.

The monotony of the candidates forced me to lose interest quickly, so I discarded the newspaper and continued walking. I picked up the pace to match the wind as the chill of the night began to descend. It was a picturesque autumn night, and I caught a glimpse of the moon floating in the pitch black sky. I finally reached Drake and fumbled to find the right key. A college was more secure than a military base; at least on a military base you could probably sneak a hooker into your bunk. Finally I found the key and jimmied the archaic stainless steel door open. The foyer of Drake Residence felt like a sauna; I immediately removed my leather jacket, and draped it over my shoulder. The Residence was silent. All I could hear was a puck hitting paddles on the air hockey table in the common room. Even the television was off, a sight which I have never witnessed before.

I hurried up the stairs, I didn't know if another night of masturbation was a reason to rush or if I simply wanted to go to sleep. Fuck. Who was I kidding? I was going to check the call display to see if Jordyn had called. We hadn't spoken in some time, and those conversations always ended with her trying to convince me to enter some deal, where we don't tell the other if we have slept with anyone. I wasn't an idiot. I knew she was with someone and just didn't want to let me in on the news. Well I guess I found the root of my misogyny. That wasn't so hard.

The door to my room was unlocked. I looked back and contemplated going back outside to have a butt. Hell, I'll just smoke it in my room. My roommates didn't mind. I entered my room; I could hear the sounds of fingers wailing away on keyboards, so I knew someone was still up, probably Luke, whose coke and XBOX addiction coupled with his love of the internet led to many sleepless nights for him. Good guy though and I always enjoyed his company. I was torn between relaxing and seeing if he was up for a late night or hitting the sack. I guess a little quality time wouldn't kill me.

I walked through the carpeted hallways, stepping softly on the light pink carpeting, with my left hand running against the white walls. I don't know when it started, but whenever I walk indoors I always touch the walls. I like the sensation of touch, of textures forcing my senses to lose that feeling of numbness you get from people. I arrived at Luke's room, a photocopy of Kurt Cobain's face hanging on his door, but I don't think

I've ever heard him listening to Nirvana. Kurt Cobain was always trendy for my generation. The wailing of the keyboard was clearly coming from his room, so I proceeded to knock. The door opened with enthusiasm, and Luke stood there. His face was pale and his nose was powdered.

"Hey, man. How was the date?" Luke said, in between sniffs to get any residue up his nose.

"Okay, I guess. It wasn't the best fifteen minutes I've ever spent, but not the worst either.

Luke spoke incredibly quickly, which is how a cokehead stereotypically talks. "Cool, cool. I'm not going to lie to you; I've been partying up in here for hours now. You want in? I got some shit from Rich today. Come taste test with me, Jack."

"Yeah alright, Luke, but you're all over the place man. You need to relax for a bit." No point in telling him what he already knows and doesn't care to hear. As I gave him my one and only pathetic plea for his own personal health, the coke smacked the cold glass coffee table, remaining intact, and exuded a gorgeous, opaque, white glow. I could see myself in it. In the reflection of the glass, I could see myself immersed in the narcotic. Cocaine was one of the better drugs, and was also easily accessible on any college campus. Weed is a close second, but the affects are not comparable. It makes you hungry, horny and anti-social. Let me tell you, horny and anti-social is the worst combination a guy could be. Ecstasy, which seemed to be the drug of choice for many of my contemporaries in high school, was a nuisance more than a high. Your jaw numbs and feels dislocated, your eyes can't follow any sight, and you can barely utter a word. Shrooms was a great phase but too much of a commitment: Four to six hours of your time in exchange for bright colors and clouds doing funny stuff. Cocaine was the way to go. You're just flying, your body loses its mass, and the entire burden you carry just disappears in one sniff. One simple little sniff.

"Alright here ya go, Jack." Luke handed me a twenty dollar bill, rolled up. I placed it in my left nostril and plugged my other nostril with my free hand. The coke flew through the bill and straight up my nose, causing my body to instantly react. My head grew lighter and all I could think about was how stupid college kids are. Most of us are here on our parents' hard earned buck, and all of that money and that stupid little degree just goes right up the nose or straight down the throat. They might as well give us the degree during frosh week, so that we can use it as papers, funnels or snorting devices.

My body had gone completely numb. I looked over at Luke who was staring aimlessly around his room. He was having trouble focusing and kept rubbing his eyes rather aggressively. I had lost all feeling in my teeth; a sober onlooker would have found my conduct rather humorous. I had to constantly touch my teeth and rub my gums to tell my brain they were all still there.

"Are Peter and Mark asleep?" I said to Luke.

"Ah, yeah Mark is sleeping at his girl's place, and Peter crashed a long time ago. Dude, I am wrecked. I've hit so many lines tonight. I am such an idiot. Just couldn't study," Luke said. His eyes were so glassy I could barely look at him.

Luke was the benchmark for mediocre students everywhere; he could rise from the streets and be their messiah. Back in first year, Peter and I had to drag him to the bookstore just to purchase course kits after classes were already a month under way. He was a behemoth as well. He hulked over me with his 6'2" frame and 215 lbs. of bulk. He was a big kid to say the least, an intimidating guy with the personality of a talkative and political teddy bear.

"Alright man, I think I am going to crash. Thanks for the hit before bed." I said to him as I got up and tried to maneuver my legs, which I felt I could no longer control. That was good coke, but it's a habit I need to drop.

"No worries, Jack. Wake me up tomorrow when you get up." Luke asked me even though I have woken him up every weekday since we got here. God, I hope he has an inheritance to fall back on some day. My head was as light as a balloon. My hormones were racing though, and I almost thought about calling Lindsay up to see if she wanted to continue our date now. I didn't have the nerve to pull those kind of moves when dealing with women.

When I arrived at my room, I felt as if I had been walking for hours, but my room is only two down from Luke's. Our Residence room was apartment-style with four separate rooms (more like little cubicles), a common room, kitchen, and one bathroom. The coke was going to wear off in forty-five minutes or so, but I still felt like a kite. Man, what an uplifting experience. I had got so caught up with getting high I forgot to check the call display. I walked over to my computer chair and quickly sat down. I leaned over and tilted my call display box towards me and began shuffling through the calls. 555-3577 didn't appear, so she hadn't called. My body was completely numb, and my brain was beginning to follow suit. I was used to this feeling, so I didn't panic. I felt numb when I was with Lindsay; and it was not a side effect from the drugs; that I was sure of. I just rested my head on my desk and let the coke take me away. I knew it would be hours before the drug would actually let me sleep.

Chapter 2

The television was blaring in the other room, and the sounds reverberated off the walls and into my room and startled me. I jumped up and rubbed my face. I felt dirty, and my head was pounding. What a stupid night. I could hear the sounds of Bob Barker sexually harassing one of those showcase girls, so I knew it was around 11:30 am. I threw my clothes off, grabbed a towel, and headed towards the shower; my roommates were not the most hygienic guys, so I was confident the shower would be free. I walked past the common room and saw Mark sitting there. I would be spending time with him soon, so I continued on my way to the bathroom.

I hopped in the shower. It was boiling hot, which I loved, and I felt the water washing the drugs out of my system. I finished up quickly. I couldn't decide if I wanted to attend class today, but if I was one of those magic eight balls I think all signs would point to no. I dried off quickly and hustled back to my room to get dressed. I was something of a morning person, so if I ever slept past nine I hustled to get ready in the morning so I could enjoy some of it. Shit, what to wear?

I got dressed and exited my room. The sunlight was shining through the window and blanketing the entire room. Mark was pretty zoned in on what was playing on the TV.

"Hey," I belted to Mark, feeling I had to be abrasive to get his attention.

"Morning, Jack. You slept in today."

"I partied with Luke for a bit last night after I got home, and then fell asleep at my desk.

"How was your date last night?" He asked in an almost nervous tone. He knew of my proficiency on dates and in most social settings.

"It was nothing to write home about. She was alright; it honestly didn't last long past the hellos. I ducked out early. I am just sick of meeting new people."

"You've always been this way, Jack. You might be the worst when it comes to women," Mark replied.

"Well…" I wanted to argue back. I was even a little insulted, but he had evidence to back up his opinion, which I just couldn't fight.

"You're a dinosaur, Jack. You have to realize that people aren't like you. Its 2004, and people, especially our generation, operate a certain way, one you just don't understand." Mark said in the friendliest tone he could use.

I pulled out a cigarette and lit it. My lungs were hurting, but the body wants what it wants. Mark hadn't told me anything I already didn't know, but I thought it was my little secret. I wasn't a dinosaur though; there were people who wanted more out of life than the vacuous lives they were already immersed in. There has to be more to life than Simon Cowell's opinion on generic aspiring singers. My generation sucks.

"Jack I am telling you, you were born in the wrong century." Mark finished up his thought, got up, and proceeded out of the room. He never liked smoke, but he dealt with it. He was also making convincing points. I think this was the longest conversation Mark and I had endured in months; I never realized I was so transparent to him. Suddenly, I remembered I had to wake up Luke. I sauntered over to his door, pounded about ten times, and told him to wake up. I had fulfilled my duty to him for the day.

I couldn't stand just sitting around my room anymore, so I grabbed my jacket and headed out the door. My roommates were used to me leaving without saying a word or having any agenda. They rarely, if ever, questioned my motives. The Drake Residence was booming. It seemed that everyone was either in the hallway or on their way out. Voices echoed throughout the halls and came together and created a tidal wave of noise.

"Jacky Boy, where you hiding these days?" I didn't recognize the voice, but she knew I heard her so there was no turning back. I turned around and saw that it was Megan. A girl I have never slept with, but wouldn't mind if the opportunity was to present itself. She was cute, with long and I mean long flowing hair, a firm body and gorgeous blue eyes. She was as Aryan-looking as one can be, and she carried with her a perfect smile.

"Busy with school and what not. You can usually find me if you wanted to," I said.

"Busy with school? You don't hear too many students say that. You're a throwback to the good old days, Jack," Megan said through all of the noise and the clutter of the hallway. I could barely hear her, but I was getting the jist of what she was saying. Maybe I was born in the wrong century, but I was lying because I wasn't busy with school at all. I just didn't know what to say. Coke has been keeping me busy, or I spend hours waiting for the ex to call? School was an honorable lie.

"I am dying for a butt and I have to go do something, but we'll hang out later," I said. We both turned away and continued on. I gave her a quick look back as I headed past the common room and out of the front door. I had a sneaking suspicion that she did the same.

I had something I wanted to do, something I had been putting off for awhile. Since I am a dinosaur or a man lost in the wrong century or whatever, this institution might identify with me. I have disagreed with just about everything they have done and continue to do, but I needed some guidance. I don't know I felt like an idiot. This place and its people made me sick to the core to be honest; I don't know why I am going here. I lit a cigarette, as I exited the building and walked down the cement stairs. There was overcast in effect, pathetic fallacy maybe, I don't know. The smoke created a cloud which hovered over me, I am sure it could be spotted from outer space, it felt thick and intrusive.

Campuses are mini-towns or self-contained communities; they encompass all student needs in the areas of education, athletics (especially athletics), shopping, food, and spiritual guidance. The lecture halls are old, dusty, and aesthetically unappealing, yet the rest of the campus looks like it was torn out of an Ikea catalogue or like a post-modern hurricane ripped through the place, destroying all tact and subtlety in its path.

I made my way through the trendy food court, which seemed to convey the true ethnicity of the student body. You could eat anything from Japanese to Greek food. The food court was always blistering with young minds, ideology, and fervor. I found that, usually, I could only withstand about fifteen minutes or my heart would break as I observed George W. Bush's youth. I kept my head down and walked through the food court, blinding and deafening myself to anyone or to any conversation that was taking place. I picked up the pace and headed towards the large flight of white and purple stairs that would lead me directly to my destination.

I arrived at the top of the stairs. I felt as if I had entered some sort of time portal. Downstairs was loud, vibrant, with nonsense bouncing off every wall and smacking every ear. Upstairs was quiet, peaceful, and almost decadent. It was a holy place and emanated that sentiment; it might have been the last untouched area of campus. Ever since I went on that campus tour prior to my freshman year, I promised myself I would visit this sanctuary, the campus Church. I don't like any devout religious person. Such people are the true dinosaurs. I especially despise the assholes who wear the excessive, gold-plated crosses and the fanatics who believe in Creation or the Evangelists who lie through their teeth. The world can do without those whores. I am not a card carrying member of any of the abrahamic religions, but I am a man who believes in God. I am more agnostic than atheist, in the sense in which T.H. Huxley originally coined the word. Atheists are liars. They say they don't believe in God, but who do they pray to when they're lying in the cold hospital bed or when their kid is missing or some shit like that? I would never deny her.

Chapter 3

After I walked all the way over, I was still reluctant to enter. People who think the umbrella of religiosity has been removed from society need to open their eyes. The campus church was small; it had about a dozen pews on each side that could sit about ten to fifteen each. It was fairly opulent though, strewn with metal crosses and dominated by stained glass windows. Churches were constructed to make you feel small in the eyes of God. This one accomplished that, and it was no bigger than a few residence rooms strung together. The carpenter or king of the Jews or whatever he is to be called hung on a cross in front of me. It was an eerie image, one which frightened me often as a child. I saw a cement bowl overflowing with "holy" water. I was going to wash my hands in it, but even alone I felt silly partaking in this ritual.

I continued walking up the aisle and sat down on the first wooden pew. I couldn't resist lighting a cigarette.

I didn't know if any priests were employed here, so maybe I would just be alone. My hands were shaking uncontrollably, which made smoking a difficult task. Did smoking in a church make me a heretic? As my eyes scanned the church from wall-to wall, thoughts of Martin Luther began to plague my mind. I mean he was an anti-Semite which I hate, but man was he brave. To look such a power as the church in the eyes, and say I have found ninety-five things wrong with you guys is simply amazing in my mind.

What was the point of us, of all of us? I mean I don't get our existence. Why do we believe in a God that has created a world full of shit? Why would a God create a species like ours? Every chance that we have had at greatness--thwarted by greed and stupidity. We rape, kill, lie, neglect each other and ourselves, and sleep around to make a fortune on which we sit until we die, and then our loved ones fight over it until they no longer speak. This vicious cycle continues for generations. Is this the great divine plan?

I continued to sit on the end of the pew. I began to recline as my cigarette burned to an end. I dropped it to the ground and stepped on it ever so softly, keeping in mind that I was in a church. The serenity was broken by a robed priest as he stepped from behind the altar. He continued walking with a sullen look on his face. He descended from the altar and motioned his finger in a way indicating that I should follow him. I wonder if he saw me smoking. It was hard not to detect. He slowly made his way over to the confessional.

I got excited. I had always wanted to go into one of those, but I figured them to be particularly outdated.

I stood up and followed the elderly priest into the confessional. He entered on the far side as I proceeded through the door closest to me.

The confessional was intimately lit and could barely fit a man my size, let alone a fat person with a guilty conscience. The little facial door slid open violently. I looked through and I could see the priest. He breathed loudly, and I didn't know if it was because he was angry with me or just old age. The holy silence was finally shattered.

"It's a dirty habit you know," said the priest, in a raspy and methodical voice.

"No more so than faith," I bellowed back. I would not waste what was potentially my only time in a confessional booth. I have so much anger towards these robed men. It couldn't contain itself.

"What are your sins?"

"What are yours?" I snapped back to him.

He threw a bewildered look at my way. His life must be filled with veneration, praise heaped upon him for choosing a life of devotion and spitting in the face of temptation. Thoughts of how many altar boys he might have raped crossed my mind.

"I am on the wrong side of the confessional to be divulging my sins. If you think that I am without because I am a priest, then you are mistaken."

"I suppose. I don't know why I came here to be honest. I detest this place. I don't understand how you can work for a corporation that wields such ignorance." I was beginning to regret trying to ruffle his feathers, he seemed nice enough.

"A corporation you say, I work for the Lord. The church is not infallible as some would have you believe. There are bad apples everywhere."

I felt some bible analogy coming my way, hitting me like a punch in the face.

"You believe in creation, Father?" I said as I sank lower into the wooden kneeler.

"Yes, I suppose I do."

"So you suppress all the facts just to prove some antiquated notion." Even as I challenged him, I felt guilty.

"Yes I do, I believe in things that exist beyond facts" He said to me.

"Ridiculous. What about the words of Jesus? You gather in this so-called sanctuary, yet Jesus himself asked his disciples to not make a show of prayer, or how do you account for the hypocrisy of the church. Fucking crusade, inquisitions, molestation, purges, c'mon man," I said to the kind priest.

My calm proved to be fleeting and my temper began to escape me. My anger built and I was trying to repress it before it rose to a crescendo. I looked for some sort of answer from this common man, even though I knew he would be unable to provide me with an adequate one. All of a sudden, the booth became hot and my clothes tightened.

"Why are you so angry?" the priest asked.

"I just can't relate, it bothers me. I don't belong here," I replied.

"Does anyone? Tell me, what are your parents like?"

"Well, my father was a lawyer but he is dead now. He passed away when I was eleven. My mom remarried a few years later. I don't know what else to say, I kind of raised myself."

"It's a little evident. You seem like a smart man, but I think you are a little too passionate. It's nice to see from someone from your generation, but I think you need to harness it. God loves you my child. Stop by again but I must be going, unless you have something to confess."

I had nothing to confess. Well, I am sure I had lots, but skeletons should remain in the closet. My closet anyways, which is full of wrong deeds, though most are victimless. I am not by any means a bad person; my noticeable flaw was a lack of tolerance for the average person.

I stood up from the kneeler and watched as the priest exited the confessional booth. He was a nice man. I felt like I was a little too hard on him and his profession. I exited the booth after awhile and walked down the aisle in between the pews out of the dimly lit church. I was happy I stopped by, and hopeful I would return.

Why do they feel compelled to tell everyone that God loves them? If you believe in God, then you believe that her love is unconditional, so why are you so insecure that you need one of her self-appointed workers to reiterate it for you? This strikes me as strange, but so does most of theology.

I exited the building and stared at the sky as I continued walking. It was always filled with such wonder. What is God's racket anyways? If she loves me, she should do my bidding, or do I do hers? Why do we waste time with prayer? We will never have any tangible proof to support the existence of a God. God should be working for us, not the other way around. I looked at the sky and kept thinking to myself, "Just please smite my enemies already."

Chapter 4

I don't know how long I was out, but when I awoke I lay in a sterilized and perfectly white room. It was almost heavenly except for the potent smell of antiseptic. I could barely move my body, as pain would shoot through my limbs. It felt as if my head had been beaten in by a band of British soccer hooligans.

"Hello Mr. Geary. How do you feel?" said an ominous voice. My vision cleared, and I saw that the voice belonged to a man who stood about two feet away from me.

"Where am I?" I replied to the stranger.

"You are in St. Augustine's hospital. You were hit by a cyclist as you were crossing a street. You were rushed here about two hours ago, and you have stabilized; we have just been waiting for you to wake up," said the man, who now I had ascertained was a doctor. Good for him, his parents must be proud.

"What's the last thing you remember? The doctor asked me.

"I was staring at the sky, and walking on asphalt and got lost in my thoughts I guess," I replied.

"And then you got hit by a cyclist, that's rough. The man who hit you just left, I better go call him and tell him you are alright," he said to me between snickers.

I didn't blame him for laughing, I am sure God was as well. God being a practical joker is a bittersweet irony we all need to accept sooner rather than later. God is omniscient, and she knows who my worst enemy truly is.

"When can I go home?"

"We'll run some tests, but you should be able to go home tomorrow," the doctor said reassuringly.

He asked me for any contacts' numbers. I gave him my roommates, and he promised me he would contact them for me. The doctor left the room, and I began moving each appendage to make sure they worked. I couldn't wait to get out of here. It's not like I had anything to do, but I don't like being stationary.

Hours upon hours passed, and then suddenly there was a knock on the door. Before I could say enter, the door swung open. Peter smiled at me as he entered and closed the door behind him. He approached the bed and pulled a chair towards it. The chair scraped along the ground with a sound I didn't enjoy. With the chair pulled up to my bed, he sat down.

"Hit by a cyclist. Wow." Peter said to me.

"Yeah isn't it a great way to go?" I replied.

"Could win you a Darwin award, hell I'd vote for you." he said as we both began to laugh. Peter was probably my oldest friend. We had met when we were in elementary school because our mothers decided to sign us up in the same carpool one year. It's not the most interesting story to tell people, but it has transformed into a solid friendship. We drifted a lot throughout high school until senior year when we got drunk together at a party. I'll never forget it. He approached me, and we began talking as if we had never lost touch. We never talked about our falling out, but, needless to say, it was over a girl.

"Doctor said you can go home today. So let's get you packed up, the other guys are excited to see you as well. Luke just hasn't been the same since the doctor called yesterday. He actually went to bed early last night."

I got out of the bed and Peter handed me a pair of jeans and a white t-shirt. I was always a simple dresser, nothing fancy or too outrageous. I walked to the bathroom, got dressed, and washed up. I was limping a bit and my body was tense and drained, the accident just knocked me out more than did any damage. I came out of the bathroom, and the two of us walked to the front desk where I signed some forms. The doctor came over one last time to make sure I was okay, and he seemed pleased enough to let me go home. I started to think if I should even tell my mom about this. I decided I'd better not. It was nothing really.

Peter and I walked over to his 1993 Mercury, which was parked right out in front of a paramedic zone. Lucky for us, it was a slow day for those guys. We hopped in and began heading back to Drake Residence.

"Thanks for picking me up," I said even though I had serious cotton mouth at the moment, and every word required an effort.

"Don't mention it. Lindsay called for you. I didn't tell her where you were, but you should give her a call Jack." He said to me without taking his eyes off the road.

"Yeah, I will, maybe even later tonight." I didn't know if I would actually call her back, but it wasn't vital to honestly answer that question right now. As we pulled into the parking lot of Drake Residence, my head began pounding and I could hear my bed calling my name. The bandages on my face and one across my nose felt as if they had lifted a bit, but I didn't care so much at the moment. Peter parked the car and we headed up to our room. I wasn't in the mood for talking, so I remained silent. We entered our room, and it was lifeless and surprisingly immaculate. It didn't sound like Luke and Mark were home, so I thanked Peter again and headed to my bed for some long needed rest.

Chapter 5

My twin bed had never felt so good. My body was mired in a perpetual state of rest. Even though I knew it was well into the evening, I didn't have any desire to get out of bed. Throughout my sleep, I had heard knocks on the door, people coming to check up on me, but I didn't feel the need to get up and answer it. I felt the need to do some drugs. It was an innate feeling, and one which was difficult to shush once it had awoken. Sometimes it got so thick that I felt the need to swat it away from my face. I knew some form of narcotics waited for me a few doors down in Luke's room if I was willing to get up. My face throbbed from the injuries I sustained when my head hit the cement. I still couldn't believe I was hit by a cyclist. There's no honor in that. Getting hit by a car, sure that's honorable, but a bicycle?

I think when I blacked out after I was hit; I saw a white light gravitating towards me. Could have just been neurons firing in my brain, or could have been an actual brush with death. I don't truly believe in our western view of heaven and hell. It seems way too tidy for a smart person to digest. St. Peter's gates, living on clouds, wings and shit like that, it just seems like some stupid fairy tale told to help average people deal with their mortality. I am positive there was something there though when I blacked out, but my memory is so fragmented it's hard to decipher what it was or if it was actually physically real. Westerners are very vulnerable to idealistic notions in regards to the issues that scare us all, I find it pretty sad.

I finally got out of bed and threw on one of my white t-shirts and a dilapidated pair of old and faded jeans. I couldn't find a pair of socks, which always seemed to be a problem of mine. I lose socks like a girl losses her virginity on prom night. I opened the door to my room and walked down the hall closing the door behind me. I opened the door to Luke's room without knocking, something I don't think I have ever done before. Luke was sitting on his bed watching television. He didn't even rotate his head to see who had just walked into his sanctuary.

"Luke, what are you up to?" I asked him.

"Just watching American Idol...please don't yell at me." He asked with his tongue firmly placed in his cheek.

"I'll make you a deal, if you can hook me up with anything right now I won't go on and on about the current state of the music industry, and how this show exemplifies the cookie cutter mentality of music and all that is currently wrong with it." I firmly asked, even though in reality I was actually begging.

"Top drawer under the post-its, but we need to save some for the Lambda party tonight." Luke said to me.

"Oh fuck that's tonight, when are we leaving?" I asked with little trace of excitement, for I was not totally enthused about going to a frat party.

"Eleven or so, make sure you are ready and no excuses from you tonight Jack. I'll take care of you fun-wise when we get there, so don't worry." Luke said to me.

He knew that I would only go to this party under certain conditions. With my accident yesterday I actually had a valid reason not to go, unlike past occasions when I would lie to them, but maybe a party would be good for my spirit. My body felt like it had been thrown through a blender. I am in horrible shape right now. Drugs I think were the only way to cure what was ailing me. I felt as if I had honestly died earlier but that could be the concussion talking. I left Luke's room and headed to the vacant common room to engage in some soul-healing.

I sat down on our white couch, which oddly enough had avoided any stains up to that point. I opened up the little white sack and emptied a little bump of cocaine on the brown wooden coffee table. I took out my MasterCard and broke it up as best I could. This was becoming a normal routine for me. I always reminded myself to use the side of the credit card without the magnetic stripe on it. The coke was broken up and was ready to do what I needed it to do. I picked up my wallet and grabbed the only bill I had left in the fold. It was a five. I wondered if I had ever done coke with a five dollar bill before, but it really didn't matter. I was happy I had a bill on me; usually I was scrambling to find something suitable. I guess you could just use a straw, but where is the cliché in that? After the bump, Luke and I rolled a small joint and smoked it to completion.

I continually wondered why Jordyn hadn't called me in so long. I knew it was because she was seeing someone else, but she could still call. I entertained the notion of calling her and telling her about my accident, and making it sound worse than it actually was. I guess this was for the best. I'll eventually find someone else, someone better, more mature, and more caring. I wasn't worried at all. I had never really had problems with women. Getting women wasn't a concern, but wanting to keep them was another story. I rolled up the bill as tight as I could until it was almost flush and the coke shot right up it and into my system, lifting me with it. My pain was superficially and temporarily gone, even though I knew I was being a reckless idiot. Jordyn always hated it when I hit lines, so I just stopped telling her when I did them. I hated a lot of the things she did, but they weren't dangerous, just little personality quirks. I lit a cigarette and placed it in my mouth. It tasted amazing. I was such a creature of habit, and my day always tended to revolve around one addiction or another. From reading to thinking to drinking to cigarettes to cocaine, I was a slave to their tantalizing powers.

The sun was beginning to set in the distance, and the shadows cast themselves into the common room and enveloped me. I began to feel cold, and my drug-induced jubilation shifted into a form of despair. I had never felt this before, and I had to hope that it would pass. I hate that feeling when you envision your own death and all you can think about is how embarrassed your mom is going to be that her baby died from a drug overdose. My emotions were all out of whack, and I needed to get out of that place and over to the party or somewhere.

I rushed over to my room stumbling into every inch of the wall on the way. My vision began to blur, and my other senses were failing me. I banged my shoulder repeatedly on different areas of the wall, and it throbbed rather vibrantly. I am an instinctive creature, and to not be able to rely on my instincts or my senses was a humbling experience. I knew the drugs would wear off eventually, that it was only a matter of time. I reached my room and fumbled through the doorway and collapsed on the carpeted floor. What is wrong with me? I thought.

I think I passed out momentarily, but it was hard to tell. I felt weak, but I was able to place my arms on the ground and lift myself up to my knees. I sat there on my knees as erect as I could in an attempt to stretch my back out, to little avail. I was still a little high from the coke, but the bad times had worn out their welcome. I coughed up an enormous ball of phlegm as I stood up. I have never had a trip like that before; I mean, I have had bad trips before but never passed out or lost control of my body like that. Thank God I had a short-term memory concerning these things. I sat at my computer desk and saw that it was already after 10 pm. It was almost time to go to the frat party. I need to get ready and drink a little and get myself into good working condition for tonight.

I placed a CD into my computer, and the music blared as I rummaged through a pile of clothes on my floor for something to wear. It was a mixed CD with everything from Bruce Springsteen to Pearl Jam to Outkast crammed into it. The music filled my room with emotions, vibes, and noise. I could hear Luke, Mark, and Peter outside my room, drinking and watching a baseball game on TV. I found a grey button up shirt and a pair of cargo pants. I put some gel on my hair, which was nothing more than a big, funeral pile of curls, but I was satisfied with myself enough to leave my room and join the festivities.

As soon as I left the room, we wasted no time in heading over to the party. We stepped outside Drake Residence and hailed the first taxi we could find. I decided not to tell Luke about my bad trip, I figured he had already tried the coke and didn't have any negative affects, so it was probably just me. I had already moved on.

I grabbed the front seat of the cab and the other three crowded into the back, having to interlock arms so that they could fit properly. As I was getting into the cab, the driver handed me something and asked me if I could discard it for him. I noticed he was handing me two empty beer bottles, but nonetheless I obliged and left them by the curb. I thought it was weird that our cab driver had been consuming alcohol, but my generation has always had this innate feeling of invincibility, so I decided to run with that.

The cab ride was short as the driver pulled in front of the frat house. We tossed him a few crumpled up dollar bills, and he seemed content, so we exited the cab and slammed the doors shut. The frat house was far too nice for a group of idiots to be renting. It was ivy-covered, and the maroon bricks were immaculate. The porch overflowed with people and the house seemed as if it would explode in some violent orgy of sex, drugs, and overpriced, flat beer.

I didn't even think we would be able to get in, but Mark ushered us through the crowd. He was a pretty big guy standing at a slender and firm 6'0". He was obsessed with working out and at times it was all he could talk about. He was always getting into Atkins or Bernstein or whatever asshole was trying to trot out some cure, to trim the fat away from America's already expanded waistline. Like I always say though, pick your poison.

We entered the labyrinth that these frat guys called home. It was four floors, and I was sure debauchery was happening on each one. It seemed like a 3:1 ratio of girls to guys, which is always a good thing for a single guy at a party. The interior in no way resembled the exterior. It was rather dilapidated even though they had state of the art entertainment devices and perfect black couches and recliners. Peter and I split off from Mark and Luke and headed over to the keg fridge. There were two girls hovering over it. One of the girls looked very familiar to me.

"Hey aren't you in my Medieval and Early Modern Europe class?" The familiar girl said as I poured some alcoholic foam into a red plastic cup.

"I guess so. What's your name?" I asked. She had one of those perfectly feminine voices.

"Alyssa Cavendish and you?" she replied.

"Jack Geary," I said in a flat tone. I think I was nervous. I still had some cuts and bruises on my face. I guess they were making me a little self-conscious.

We continued having small talk for a bit, and then I suggested that we go to get some fresh air. I know when a guy says that it is implied that he is hitting on her, but I really just needed some fresh air. Peter had already walked off with a beer in each hand, and I hadn't seen the other two in a little while. I filled my plastic cup up to the brim once again, and placed my hand on the small of Alyssa's back as we headed towards the front door. As we walked through the house, I saw Lindsay talking to some guy wearing frat letters on his sweatshirt. I figured I should steer clear of her in order to avoid any awkwardness.

We walked outside, right into a cloud of smoke. Not going to lie to you, it was an appealing smell to me. I knew the time to enter into some inane banter was upon me. Alyssa chugged her beer rather ladylike and licked the froth off of her upper lip.

"So, Jack what are you going to do with a history degree when all is said and done?" Alyssa asked me.

"I want to write a novel. I don't know how a history degree will help me. I think I have that one great book in me," I replied, trying my best not to sound glib.

"What kind of novel would you write?" she asked.

"My goal is just to write a novel that provokes some guy to kill a celebrity or politician." I couldn't contain my little smirk after sharing my aspiration with Alyssa. This really was a dream of mine. I mean, whenever some tragedy befalls society, some movie, band, or artist is always blamed. I just figure if I was to ever write a book that resulted in an assassination, I would make it easy on society to scapegoat me. Let's be honest though, J.D. Salinger didn't kill John Lennon, and no Keanu Reeves movie resulted in Columbine. The asshole politicians who point fingers at the arts need to start taking accountability and dish some on to the blind parents.

"That is really odd, Jack," Alyssa said even though I could tell she was smart enough to catch my point. I continued sipping my beer. My face was still numb from the accident, and I was completely beat. I felt half alive and my entire brain was drained. At least this was the first time, I had flirted with a girl without thinking about Jordyn. Alyssa was stunning and seemed intelligent. Her short brown hair and her dark eyes were a perfect match. I thought maybe I could swing this if I played my cards right. Who was I kidding? I was playing poker with my cards facing out, but I knew I had nothing to lose.

"There is a ton of people out here any chance that we could go somewhere more quiet?" I asked, trying to act my most confident.

"Absolutely. Let's go find a free room or corner or something."

Alyssa grabbed my hand, and I followed her back into the obnoxiously loud house. I had been leaning up against the house outside. I noticed some of the ivy had gotten onto my shirt. I was getting excited; I would welcome any intimacy from an intelligent woman. She walked at a quick pace; the faster she walked, the harder she would grip my hand. We continued through the busy house, we passed by various students all of whom seemed drunk. The house was buzzing with conversations and there was a kinetic vibe flowing throughout the dwelling. As we walked, I caught a glimpse of Lindsay talking to a different guy now, and I also saw Peter who locked eyes with me for a quick second until he returned back to his conversation. Alyssa led me up a spiraling staircase to the third floor of the house. The hallway upstairs was quiet with only the muffled sounds of the noise downstairs echoing up to us. Alyssa knocked on one door and when no one answered, she turned the doorknob only to find it locked. I hadn't uttered a word yet because I hadn't been in this situation for awhile. Alyssa proceeded further down the hall to the next door.

I guess Alyssa was too preoccupied to hear the voices coming from inside, but I was keen enough to notice them. It didn't sound pleasant. Alyssa swung the door open, and rushed us inside. Our excitement was permanently replaced by shock. The room was dimly lit but the action taking place was unmistakable. He was an enormous man and was draped all over her. I couldn't make out either of their faces, but something about this situation wasn't right. Alyssa yelped and ran out of the room from embarrassment. I think she was expecting me to follow suit, but my feet felt like they were nailed to the wooden floor. The man got off of the young girl, as he did, the girl turned her head towards me. I noticed who she was and my heart began to crack. It was Megan. I looked over at Megan as she was bent over with her face uncomfortably pushed into a pillow. I could see tears streaming down her face, mixing with makeup to create the face of a very tortured girl. The man got up from his kneeling position and pulled his pants up. He walked over to where I stood and reached over to shut the door. The man grabbed me by the neck and threw me up against the corner. He smacked my face with a calloused fist, and enforced the pre-existing throbbing I was already experiencing. He breathed so loud that I could barely hear myself think. He punched me two or three times. I couldn't count. It didn't matter to me. As he loomed over me, I kept looking towards Megan. She was broken, and blood was covering her upper thighs, dripping onto the sheets of the bed. It was awful, all of my misogyny had transformed into empathy in one swift punch, empathy for a young girl whose life would never be the same. The look in her eyes was telling me that she knew her fate as well.

I could see past the fratboy (who was wearing a shirt with Greek letters on it), and could tell that Megan was slowly working up the courage to get up. I was trying to signal to her to not worry about me and just to run, but unfortunately there isn't a universal sign for that. Blood was pouring out of my face and over my eyes, and I could no longer see. Megan got up quietly and ran passed us and out of the room. The fratboy finally cared enough to notice that she was gone.

He gathered his belongings, which were on the night table. I could hear voices outside of the room, and no one seemed alarmed by the distraught girl who just ran out of the room. The banal conversations pressed forward like weary soldiers engaged in battle. I placed my tender ear up to the wall and could actually feel the apathy flowing from their mouths and through the wall into my ear. I removed my ear from the cold wall, and dropped my head down to stare at the puddle of blood that had accumulated on the floor. "Don't ever repeat this," he said as he left the room. The pain in my face was unbearable. I continued to sit in the corner with my arm resting on one knee. I figured if I left the room looking like this it would arouse suspicion. I didn't want Mark, Luke, or Peter to see me. I hope Megan had enough sense to go to the hospital or to the police or somewhere that gives you a false sense of security. I can't believe guys like that fratboy actually exist. Why is one person's orgasm more important than another's innocence? I continued to sit and think as the blood on my clothes and face dried up.

Chapter 6

I finally got myself off of the floor and out of my own personal puddle of blood. I decided I would casually walk out of this party and hoped anyone who noticed wouldn't care to ask what happened. I was fairly certain that the fratboy had left by now but then again he didn't seem like the most logical guy I had ever encountered. I just kept thinking how stereotypes can sometimes actually ring true, such as, a frat boy committing date rape. I mean, what an unoriginal bastard.

I was surprisingly calm and collected as I exited the house. What was not surprising was how all of my peers were too busy answering their cell phones or trying to get laid to notice a guy bleeding to death. I could only imagine the look on their sober faces the next morning as they tried to figure out where the trail of blood led to. This thought actually made me laugh, until I noticed that laughing hurt my now tender ribs. I had become a punching bag for this institution of higher education. First they drain your wallet, then, through one circumstance or another, they try to remove all blood from your system.

The thought of hailing a cab crossed my mind, but I figured I needed the walk to clear my head. If it was a five minute cab ride, it couldn't have been that long of a walk anyways. I kept contemplating whether I was some sort of hero, but I couldn't wrap my mind around that notion, so I let it fade into obscurity. All in all, it was still a pretty good party until that horrible incident. As I continued walking through the student ghetto back to Drake, I raced through my memory as I was curious whether I had ever bled this much in my life. My face was like a geyser, unleashed and uninhibited. I was surprised I was not weaker from having lost so much blood but I guess my adrenaline was flowing rather freely. Man, that fratboy is going to be one hell of a teamster one day.

I walked through the student ghetto, which featured nicer homes than most yuppies could ever dream of owning. Most of the homes were semi-detached and newly built or renovated. They mimicked suburbia in their symmetry and similar appearances; it was almost blinding to look at their unified monotony. I was happy I didn't live in one of those overpriced, postmodern dwellings. They just seemed so impersonal and distant. We already live life as if we are all bubble boys and girls, barely interacting with anyone intimately outside of sex. Whatever happened to the cozy home? How did it become outdated? One day, somebody will have to sit me down and explain to me what exactly progress is, because I didn't see it anywhere I look.

I looked back and noticed that my trail of blood had stopped a long time ago. I felt that this was a good sign. I would feel better as soon as I could clean myself up. I thought it would be a good idea to burn these clothes instead of washing them. Bad memories tend not to wash away. They cling and cling and permeate themselves into your life until you are suffocated.

I was finally on campus, and the smells and sights were becoming familiar to me. The campus was dead, but I could hear rustling in the background in the campus bars. It was Friday and students were trying to forget everything they learned in the past week. The Hound was thriving tonight. I could have used a stiff drink, but I didn't think I was in any condition to be a patron in any establishment right now. I figured out of sight, out of mind would be my best course of action right now, so I placed my eyes squarely on the concrete and sped up the already brisk pace of my walking. I arrived at Drake Residence and grabbed the swinging door before it shut as a girl was passing through it. She gave me a long look and I could feel the sympathy in her eyes. She knew I had been hurt, but she continued on her way, trying not to be invasive. As I walked into Drake, I realized how silent and still it was. Not even a single sound echoed throughout the entire building. I rushed up the empty staircase and hurried into my room, which we left unlocked from when we originally left for the party. I let the door close itself behind me and ran to the bathroom. I didn't want to get blood on the carpet or furniture, because I knew that Mark would have had my head on a pike. I brushed my teeth vigorously and watched as my blood mixed with tap water and slid down the drain. I watched it for a few seconds until the water was completely clear. I rinsed my face and ran water through my curly hair. I stopped to catch my breath and stared at myself in the mirror. I could see a possible black eye forming, my left cheekbone was completely red, and my face looked flushed. I could barely recognize myself in the mirror.

I decided to hold off showering until I could relax for a bit. I exited the bathroom and limped over to my room. The door was cracked slightly open, and I placed my hand on the doorknob and pushed it open some more. My desk lamp was on, and as I scanned the room I saw a figure lying in my bed. It was a sweet figure, who displayed a strong silhouette on my wall. She was asleep, and I could hear her breathing rather heavily. So unfair that she would have to go through something like this. No one should have to be treated like all they have to offer is their sexual organs.

I met Megan on the first day of school back in first year, right after I had moved in. We didn't hang out much, nothing more than the odd pleasantry in the hall or some generic drunk flirting. She always appealed to me though, her personality and the way she carried herself. She wasn't your average American nineteen-year-old girl; she was sincere. Why didn't I get to know her better in the past year and a half? I took time out of my night to have a drink with Lindsay, but I couldn't spend fifteen minutes with Megan.

She looked so fragile. Even before this incident she always had this air of tranquility. She was my height and completely unthreatening to anyone, and I loved the way her hair curled unassumingly in front of her face. She had blonde hair which accentuated her full face. I couldn't take my eyes off of her where she was curled up in the fetal position on my bed. She didn't even remove the cover when she sought refuge in my room. She had gotten some blood on my bed, which normally would freak me out, but it didn't seem to bother me right then. How could somebody hurt her? She would never harm anyone. The thought of someone forcing themselves inside her as she begged them to stop, made me violently angry. The event of that night raised too many questions that would go unanswered.

"Come lie down, Jack," She said to me without even turning her head.

I didn't answer her back, but I took my shoes off and lay behind her. The room was completely silent except for the sounds of our hearts palpitating and thoughts racing through my head. She was curled so tight I didn't know where I should place myself in regards to her. I didn't feel that this was the time to invade any of her personal space. At the same time, the inches between our bodies made me feel like I was light years away from her. I wanted to collapse that space so badly. She tried to hide her tears from me by muffling them in my pillow. I wanted to explain to her that karma works itself out or some shit like that, but nothing I could say could possibly erase what happened to her tonight.

I lay next to her still body and placed my arm over her waist. I didn't want it to be sexual; I wanted it to be affirming. She gripped my arm with her hand, and we just lay there. I didn't move. I contemplated whispering something in her ear, but decided against it.

After a while, she stopped crying and drifted into sleep. I couldn't sleep so I just lay there, replaying the night over and over again in my cracked head. I heard my roommates come home, but I didn't greet them. I just continued to lie there and stared at the back of Megan's head. I was happy she was getting some much needed rest; she looked calm.

Once again, God had left the species that she had created to fend for their own well being. She chose to abstain from protecting her loved ones from harm. How can we believe in a deity that would do this? But in the same breath you have to ask yourself how you can not believe in her. Theology always dictates how God tests the ones she loves. Blacks and Jews are loved, because supposedly they are the chosen ones. God rarely test the wealthy, the elite, or the ignorant. She will never waste her time with the greedy CEO or the deceitful politician or the rapist or child molester. God has no use for them and doesn't care how they stand up to adversity. They are born, they live, they hurt, and they will be forgotten in the eyes of God.

This thought took hostage of my brain and gave me comfort as I watched Megan breathe calmly in and out. Her chest moved in a rhythmic manner. I decided that I needed to go see the priest tomorrow. I would leave early, hopefully before Megan woke up and I would head quietly over to the campus church to vent. My room was completely silent and still. It was almost eerie, but it relaxed my aching body and allowed my brain to shut itself off and not worry about her or myself. The questions of that night and all of the metaphysical jargon that was running a marathon in my mind would have to rest for now. I couldn't handle the stampede at the moment and finally my eyes shut and the pain was temporarily gone.

Chapter 7

Morning came and my eyes popped open as if they knew I had business to take care of. To my dismay Megan was not in my bed anymore, but I didn't fret since I figured I was of some help to her through what was probably the worst night of her life. There were still stains of blood on my body from the beating I had endured the night before, so I removed all of my clothes and immediately headed towards the bathroom for a long overdue shower.

After my shower I was eager to get going, so I threw on the first shirt and pair of pants I could find. I didn't even bother trying to find socks. My roommates were still asleep, so I was extra quiet while making my breakfast. It was utterly morbid out as the rain was pouring from the sky and flooding the ground. The conditions outside made the room almost pitch black. I had to turn on all of the lights just to see what I was doing. I tossed two eggs, some mushrooms and green onions in a pan and some bacon in another one and waited for the results. I rushed through my breakfast, almost excited to see if the priest would have any insights for me today. I had enjoyed our last conversation, and I almost regretted my preconceived notions about him and all priests. I still had a deep hatred of the Church, but this priest seemed different, he wasn't cramming any crap down my throat, and he seemed fairly non-judgmental. The way he spoke was not as if he was lecturing from some perch, but he realized he was just a man simply wearing a robe.

I threw my dish in the already full sink and wiped the grease on my hands onto my pants, which I can almost guarantee were already dirty. I whipped my jacket around my shoulders and let it settle on my upper body, and then I tossed a winter hat on my head and walked towards the door. As I was about to walk down the stairs, I looked over to Megan's room and wondered if she was there. If I was her, I would have just packed it up and gone home. I don't know her too well, but she seemed like someone who would just repress an incident like a date rape until her hair turned gray and she developed a stutter. I took one step towards her room, but figured she needed her space, and, if she needed me again, she knew where to find me. I walked gingerly down the stairs. I left the building and instantly became frigid from the awful weather. This was not a typical autumn day; it seemed more like one of those legendary Canadian winters everyone talks about. I lifted the collar of my jacket in a pathetic attempt to keep the wind-chill off of my delicate face.

I entered the Student Center and walked up the stairs towards the church. The entire building was completely empty, most likely because of the dreadful weather. I stood in front of the open thick doors of the small church. It was warmer than the rest of the building. It was empty as always, and I walked down the aisle and sat on the same pew where I had last time. I lit a cigarette hoping to alert the priest that I had arrived. I wondered if he would ask me what happened to my face. I am sure that he heard some guy was hit by a cyclist outside of where he works; it was good fodder for ecclesiastical water cooler talk. I am also certain that if he matched the times up he could ascertain that maybe it was me, but then he might disregard it as too unlikely.

The smoke from my cigarette filled the air, elevating all of the way to the hanging cross on the ceiling. I smoked quickly in a weird attempt to help digest my breakfast. I think that is the reason I eat, because a cigarette tastes so good afterwards. I am such a sad bastard. My eyes were fixed on the immaculate parquet floor, and I reclined in my seat to relax my muscles. I felt tense and annoyed. This was easily the most active and negative week of my life. I thought back to the day my father died and how that was a bad week as well. This felt worse though, I guess it was just from the circumstances. I have always been able to accept death, even when it is that of a loved one. There's rarely anyone to blame for this shit, so you might as well just begin the healing process as soon as you can. Maybe I am strong or maybe I am too empty to grieve like the rest, but I heal quickly inside and out, as my appearance from the neck up could somewhat attest to.

The small church began to soothe me as it had the previous time that I had visited. I began to wonder where the priest was. I didn't hear any rustling in the back or anywhere around the church for that matter. I don't think holy men get days off or vacation time, which begs the question why they don't start a union so that they could get a few more job perks. The joke of a union boss in a meeting with the Pope and some cardinals, trying to iron out a collective bargaining agreement simply writes itself.

I should have told Megan to come with me to visit the priest to talk with him; he might be able to help her. Spiritual guidance can't hurt someone who has just been torn apart from the inside and left on the side of the road to die. I really hope she went to the police. The case files of fratboys' rape victims must fill an entire filing cabinet. Where do those guys get off thinking they can hurt someone the way they do? How have women become nothing more than walking sexual gratification to us? I couldn't even fathom the thought that a week ago I had soured on women.

Suddenly, while I sat on the pew, lost in the abyss of my own thoughts, a hand found its way onto my shoulder.

"I had a feeling you were the victim of a careless bicycle," said the familiar voice.

"How did you know?" I replied without even turning around.

"You wanted some sign from God. You wanted to validate your anger so he let you."

"She doesn't really work in mysterious ways then. She seems transparent to me." I said hoping he would notice the contrast of how we refer to the same God, even though he is aware that she goes by ninety-nine different names. I turned and gazed at him. The first time I met him, it was hard to get a solid look at his appearance. The confessional booth wasn't perfectly lit and prior to that he was standing at a distance from where I had been sitting. Now he was right in front of me, and I could see exactly what he looked like. He was a middle-aged man; I would make an educated guess and say that he was pushing sixty or so. He had lost a bit of hair and his belt was almost buckling from his weight. The unfortunate side effect of age forced him to squint just to see me, who was merely a few feet away from him. He had a kind face; it was a face that most would refer to as "a face with character."

He walked away from me and into the confessional booth. I followed him into it and knelt down as comfortably as I could, but my knees instantaneously began to ache. Every valley of my body had endured too much the past few days. I really need some sort of vacation from this place. The door in the little confessional slid open and once again I had trouble making out the priest's face.

"So I never see you in here in all the years that I have run this chapel, and now I see you twice in one week, Jack," the priest said.

"I need help. This week has been very unsettling to me. I saw something that, I don't know, changed me. I feel different. Even though what I witnessed did not surprise me, it's how I expect people to act," I said to the kind priest. I thought back to the night before, and the look on Megan's face. I remembered how powerless she was. He could have gone on all night if he wanted to. Every time one of the bruises on my face began to throb, my mind flooded with memories of Megan's horror. The priest waited for me to say something more; he was staring at me, potentially wondering why there were so many bruises on my face.

"I walked in on my friend being raped last night," I said to him, unable to look him directly in the eyes.

"That's awful. Does it also explain the bruises on your face?"

"Not entirely."

"Did you go to the police?" he said to me in a frank tone.

"No, it wouldn't make a difference. Don't give me shit about it. It's the way things work. I've accepted it, and she will eventually as well," I replied, saddened by the reality of the world we live in, where a girl getting raped is so common place it rarely surprises anyone. Women are underappreciated, men are allowed to run wild, and it's a bad equation. I never understood why when women are victimized we tell them not to walk the streets alone at night; when it's the men who should be chaperoned. Fine, maybe this is a generalization, but if I can open the newspaper one day and not find an article where a woman was stripped of her self-respect from a man on a power trip or not charming enough to get a woman into bed, I would be a happy guy.

The priest placed his hand on his face, searching for the right thing to say. I am sure he was racking his brain for some biblical passage or story which exemplified the moral of my experience. I waited patiently for him to form the sentence in his head, and for it to travel through his mouth and into my ear to make me feel better.

"How is she?" the priest finally said. This was the best he could do, assuming if she was dead, I would not be here. If she was in the hospital, I would not be here, so she is fine. I am less than pleased with this visit so far.

"She's fine. She is rattled, but she'll make it," I said to him angrily.

"Is she strong?"

"I don't know her that well to be honest, but I guess time will heal her." I grew angrier at his lack of insight into the situation. I needed guidance, not a question and answer period. I could have had this conversation with one of my roommates. I came to him for healing or for some answers.

"There are people in this world who are selfish, who will hurt others without giving any thought to it. Not that any rational thought could justify it. The world is not a bad place; it is just littered with a few bad apples. For every person who rapes another, there are thousands of people who don't bother a soul and just go about their lives," said the priest, and I realized he was right, but nonetheless this theory didn't make the reality any easier to swallow. My mind began to drift during the silence. I need to get out of this place. I had only been here for a year and a few months but it was beginning to wear on me. I haven't been to classes all week, and the people were so vapid and grating.

"I think I am going to bring her to speak to you," I said to the priest.

"Please do, I would love to meet her and help her. I think you need some help as well, Jack. You need to get yourself together. You have seemed so flustered both of the times I have seen you."

I stared at the floor and finally stood up. I didn't feel it necessary to say anything so I just proceeded out of the confessional and out of the church. I looked back and didn't see the priest leave. I hope he wasn't offended by my quick exit.

I never got the answers I wanted when I went to that place. It was tranquil and a bit haunting. It fit my personality to a tee and I felt at home in it. I didn't know what to do with the rest of my day, but what are you supposed to do the day after you witness a rape?

I continued walking down the street, past the spot where I was hit by a cyclist a few days earlier. I couldn't help but let out a little laugh when I cautiously looked both ways before I tempted fate by venturing across the street again. I was starving, so I headed in the direction of The Hound to grab a drink and a bite to eat. The campus was beginning to bustle. People huddled together in the student centre for some pointless protest. I was going to go when I originally heard about it a week ago via a flyer placed on the handle of my door. I figured it was a waste of time. Political change takes a lifetime of commitment and work, it is not like infamy where in one afternoon you can fly a plane into a building and be remembered forever. People are always so willing to shave their heads or get a swastika tattoo, but, hell, no one will sacrifice their lives to make the world a better place. It is a fucking sad state of affairs.

The protest was for the right to free speech, which the university was always more than willing to stifle. I can't remember the incident which brought on the protests, but these students were in so far over their heads they might as well pack it in and go home. They had the power and could easily force some kind of reform, but it would take more than one weekend to achieve, and they wouldn't commit more time to it.

Most of these kids were here on their parents' buck. They usually just kept their mouths shut, did their time, and called it an education. I tried to pay my own way from the day I entered high school against the wishes of my deceased father's will. I stopped and looked over at the protest and tried to make out what the person with the megaphone was saying. It was completely muffled, which I found slightly ironic. The crowd was multicultural, which was nice to see; yet, instead of chanting anything in unison, they carried on private conversations amongst themselves in little cliques.

Protesting must make them feel important as they try to exercise their political voice. The only problem we face is we don't have a collective voice. We have no understanding of war or any kind of real economic struggle. We consume and spend and turn a blind eye to what is really going on in the world. We simply and frivolously waste day after day and dollar after dollar.

I continued walking past the protest wondering how they sought to achieve their goals today. Eventually they will realize their meager attempts are futile. I really hope I don't sound preachy when I speak aloud. When I am in my head, my moral system is the law of the land. I love being in my climate-controlled head, but being here at this school with these people was beginning to force me to spend too much time looking inward. I was becoming a fragment of something I hated, and I was growing tired of being angry all of the time.

I should have just dropped out of school and bought a ticket to somewhere in Europe. I could have spent a semester abroad, but I didn't think I had the grades for it. I needed to get out of this place as it had begun to envelop me. Thoughts were circling my mind about maybe going home for a bit, but I couldn't have at that point. My mom basically forced me to leave. I know she missed me, but it was not the best situation. I know you can't run from your problems. They are the emotional equivalent to your shadow; they will follow you everywhere and will never subside. I have never been one to back down from a fight, even if the opponent was I.

The campus was incredibly busy now. It felt like everyone was moving in fast forward with some sort of agenda. I walked passed numerous brick walls, which were covered in colorful graffiti. The statement, "INDIFFERENCE KILLS", was painted all over the brown bricks. I finally arrived at The Hound and was eager to sit down. It was relatively full, but I was able to grab a booth by the bar all to myself. I sat down on the plush, red cushion and placed my jacket on the rack next to my booth. I relaxed for a bit and was starting to feel pretty good. My body felt loose and uncoiled. I was known for my horrible posture, so it felt nice to let my body rest in its proper form with my back straight and my feet placed firmly on the ground. I was starving so I reached to the center of my table and grabbed the menu.

I looked across the bar and my field of vision became flooded with so many different faces and bodies. I don't think there was one female navel covered in the whole joint. If I had been in this position a week ago, I would have seen all of these women as merely two-dimensional, but my vision was clearer now. I saw through crystal lenses, the undercoat of this university and what transpires here. It is a meat market, constantly on display, a human auction where women are harvested and sold by the pound.

The waitress arrived at my table, and I placed my order, completely ignoring the smile she had thrown my way. I was absolutely starving, and I could feel a void in my stomach. My body was still sore, and I had trouble sitting still because of the pain shooting mildly from limb to limb, but I had no choice but to sit until I got some food in my system.

The waitress promptly brought me a steak sandwich with fried onions, barbecue sauce, and a side of fries. It was delicious, but I ate it so fast I could barely taste it. I asked for the bill at the same time, so I could leave immediately after I finished eating. The bill came to just over nine dollars, so I left her a sizable tip, grabbed my jacket and headed out of The Hound, past all of the noise and exposed stomachs. Once outside, I could not resist lighting a cigarette. My throat was scratchy, but I took it down with relative ease and it was all worth it once the fire got going.

I was always a spontaneous person, and this running away notion was really occupying my mind. I headed in the direction of the academic advisor's office to see if I could defer my credits, anything to get away from this cesspool. Australia would be amazing, or France--Hell, I would take a semester on a farm in southern Ontario if it meant peace and quiet. I cannot remember a time when the campus was so beaming with life. It was everywhere you looked. I recognized a few faces but for the most part I felt like an outsider or the proverbial fly on the wall.

I consistently overheard conversations of how wasted people got and how stupid they behave when they do so. It was like I never left high school. What a feeling, I kept thinking to myself. This is the educational elite of America…right here, right in front of me. As I walked down this path of this college, I observed the future politicians, lawyers, doctors, and CEOs that would forge the new path and vision of America.

Sadness crept into my gut and spread like a cancer through my body. I felt it about to pour out of my orifices unless I stopped thinking about the future of this country. Greece. I could hide in Greece for a few months. This would take a lot of planning that I was just not use to, but if I could pull it off, I could change everything for myself.

After being lost in my thoughts for awhile, a familiar face appeared.

"Geary, hey! Over here." A male voice hailed to me from point blank range, piercing my eardrum. I turned my head and saw Adam standing near the crowd talking to some students. Adam was a friend of mine from high school, who I have been meaning to run into at some point. I forgot about Adam due to the chaos that occurred at the beginning of every college year. Adam was a diminutive man whose red hair gave the impression from far away that his head was actually on fire. He was as scrawny as they came. I remember I met him through Luke, who had befriended him in a grade ten drama class. He was part of our group, but it always seemed like he never felt as if he fit in. He wasn't really into drugs, and girls never seemed to notice him much. His parents owned an amazing cottage on a private resort property, to which we always convinced him to let us escape to whenever the weather warmed. We have been back at college for months now and he hasn't even been to our room. I saw him standing around two or three other guys. I was happy he had met some people.

"Geary where the hell have you been? I haven't seen you since last semester during exams. I am having the craziest year so far, a lot better than my freshman year. I have been meaning to see you guys. How are the guys doing? How's Luke?" Adam said to me without taking a single breath.

"I am glad you are getting by. The guys are great. Luke is—Luke. Nothing has changed with him. This semester in college has been decent, not as good as freshmen year though. I might be splitting though, going overseas or something for a bit." I decided I might as well let him in on my new revelation. I procrastinate like it was going out of style, but I think I could pull this off. I don't think telling people will come back to bite me in the ass.

"You'll never change, Geary. Can't stay put for a second. I am happy for you, but I think your priorities are all out of whack. Hey, we haven't seen each other in a while, so I'm not going to give you any shit," Adam said before he was interrupted by some guy trying to get him to sign some petition. Adam seemed heavily involved in the neo-protests going on today. I found this thought hilarious because I knew what a socially unaware person Adam truly was.

"Geary I have to get back to some guys I left, but let's meet at The Hound tomorrow for a drink, bring Luke with you. I'll be there after nine or so." Adam didn't even wait for a response before scurrying away. I watched him for a moment but then lost him in some large crowd. I wasn't surprised since he was never the type to stand out. I started to reminisce about high school and those weekends up at Adam's cottage. I would always anticipate them, and the five of us would always go full out for those three or four days. Adam would watch us do drugs and swap stories about our latest sexual endeavor. I was always the most introverted out of the group, so I would mainly pay attention to Mark, Luke, and Peter talk as if their lives revolved around some girl who was drunk enough to buy their bullshit at some bar.

I headed towards the south end of campus where the crowd began to thin out considerably. For almost a full minute I could walk without being bombarded with overpriced designer clothes, cookie cutter chatter, and pierced body parts that had no business being pierced in the first place. I headed up a long flight of cement stairs that lead to a roof that overlooked the entire campus. I swung open a door and marched inside straight into the office of the academic advisor.

I approached the desk and saw a middle-aged woman sitting at her desk having about fifteen different conversations at one time over the telephone. Why they don't hire more receptionists is beyond me. Poor woman, is her eight bucks an hour really worth it? They probably slashed her HMO as much as they could during the last set of cutbacks. This woman looked as if she had just survived a nuclear holocaust. Her red hair was ruffled, and her makeup looked as if a straight man had applied it on her. She impatiently tapped her pen in front of the keyboard of her computer, which looked so old it could have been the prototype.

"Can I just ask you a quick question?" I said trying to be as polite as possible. It didn't do any good. She just raised her finger, signaling to hold on for another minute.

"What do you need?" she whispered to me as she covered the mouthpiece of the phone.

"All I want is info on doing a semester abroad."

"Here, take this," she said as she rifled through her drawer of miscellaneous crap to fetch me some faint yellow flyer.

"This is for a seminar on doing a semester abroad. Just show up to that room on that date, and they'll address anything you need to know," she said to me and then continued with her phone conversation. It sounded like she was getting berated. I looked at the unprofessionally-made flyer and headed out of the office. The seminar was not for another week or so, which should give me time to figure some things out beforehand and maybe even attend some classes.

Chapter 8

My goal for the week was to attend at least half of my classes. I am surprised at myself because I know how important education is; I look down on my friends who chose to work at a gas station instead of going into even the most remedial college program. I was enrolled in five courses, and I had attended only a handful of lectures per course, but this week I would go and soak it all in. I would be a student... I would be number 27003361 as I am known by the administration of this esteemed college.

I was up and out of bed by seven in the morning. I diligently packed my books (a total of $600 USD) and course kits (a total of $350 USD) into my school bag and headed towards the living room. I felt refreshed and responsible. Something was stirring inside of me. The Megan incident might have been the darkness before the dawn or some crap like that.

I made myself a small breakfast, which consisted merely of processed cheese on a bagel and a cup of coffee. I needed to do laundry, but luckily for me I was able to find some clean clothes in a bottom drawer in my closet.

I had to check my schedule to see where I was going, and then I headed out the door to attend my eight o'clock lecture in Durbin Hall. I stepped outside. Even though it was so early in the morning, it was comfortably hot outside. The campus was dead, which didn't surprise me at all. Even most of the shops and restaurants were closed still. My back was not used to supporting this kind of weight, and I had to constantly shift shoulders to ease the pain. I finally saw another student, but he walked right past me. He was lost in the sounds emanating from his MP3 player. His hair was grungy and fingernails were black. Fishnet covered his forearms. He stared at the ground as if he was trying to decode some type of message hidden in the concrete. He looked angry but in a suburban kind of way, where he is only angry because he hasn't had any real adversity in life, unlike some of his heroes. If anything, my generation should be throwing daily parades for the blessings we have been given, the lack of tests and obstacles. We walk on rose petals and snowboard through life and then if one little thing goes wrong, all of a sudden there is a crack in the earth.

I thought to myself how weird of a notion it is to reject happiness, to not want to be happy because it is boring or unromantic. Depression has become this ideal state, bursting with appeal, which draws people into its web. I walk around the campus, and I see silver spoons driving in their Lexuses, scowling at the world. I can be bothered by the state of the world or by the consequences of history, whereas these assholes are upset because it is trendy. If only pop music could reflect how I really feel.

I entered into Durbin Hall and straight towards lecture hall C. It was close to eight, so I looked through the window and saw a few people already seated. I entered the theater and headed up the stairs to the back row and had a seat. I looked around my spacious surroundings and saw only about a dozen people sitting down; the majority were men reading the newspaper.

The theater was large but felt cramped as the seats were only inches from each other. I placed my jacket on the seat next to me, hoping it would deter people from sitting in that chair. The lecture theater was drafty, and its cement walls looked more stained yellow than painted with a large, white, PowerPoint screen facing the class. It was not a welcoming room, and it didn't seem like a comfortable learning environment. It strikes me as odd that when designing these places they didn't take that into consideration. Where do they find these decision-making, bureaucratic assholes anyways?

The lecture hall began to fill up as mainly freshmen began entering through the wooden doorway and up the aisles. One plastic young adult after another, posing as a student pretending to care, entered lifelessly with their electronics acting as extensions of their appendages. MP3 players and cell phones were extensions of one's ears, palm pilots extensions of one's hands, and electronic notebooks extensions of one's eyes. It was a sight to see to watch these cyborgs enter into a lecture hall where we learn about history, philosophy, and politics. My plan proved futile. I became sandwiched between two extremely overly dressed, chatty freshmen girls. I thought for a second that maybe I should switch seats with one of them, but, as I was contemplating that, the lecture began, and silence fell across the theater.

The professor had the appearance of a stereotypical professor. Stereotypes aren't born out of thin air; they are conceived over many similar observations. He was well under six feet tall with an awkward hunch about him and an obvious comb over. His glasses constantly slipped to the end of his nose, and he seemed annoyed to always have to be pushing them back up to the top of his nose near his squinty eyes. He spoke in a deliberate and forceful manner and was fond of enunciating every single syllable of every word. He was concise in his speech and had a jerky flare to the way he moved. When he turned his back to the class to walk towards the chalkboard, he could have been mistaken for a bald, fat Charlie Chaplin.

He carried on about the barbarian invasions of Rome and was successful in completely sucking all life out of its inherent excitement. He displayed on maps where these tribes came from and where they finally settled, omitting all of the pillaging and plundering that went on in between. It's a shame because the pillaging and plundering is something my generation could actually relate to. We have been raping our parents and the economy since we were given our first charge cards. We are the modern barbarians. As opposed to "the unshaven ones," we are plastic and porcelain. Yet, we serve the same purpose. The clique tribes, if you will. Instead of Attila the Hun, we are led by the likes of Britney Spears and George W. Bush through the valleys, over the mountains in order to claim what we feel is truly ours.

The girls on both sides of me kept leaning back and quietly carrying on meaningless conversations. I found this annoying and could see that the TA sitting in our row was not appreciative of it either. Their bubble gum filled mouths, highlighted hair, and high boots made stark contrast with the information conveyed in this course. We learned of the crusades and Christendom, and they snapped their gum and literally spoke of new ways to lose weight without having to give up gorging. The guys in front of me appeared just as frivolous and airy as the girls. It might have been fate which brought them all together in this lecture hall. I looked over at the pieces of blank paper in front of them and wondered why they would prefer to play games on their cell phones to jotting down a few facts. Of course, as I said this I realized I had not truly absorbed a single thing that the professor had uttered in the first twenty minutes of the class.

I flipped through my notebook and began feverishly writing down points from the sentences that were echoing through the lecture hall. This was short-lived because as I was about to begin my third line of writing, a dainty, frail finger tapped me gently on my left shoulder from the seats behind me. I quickly turned around and saw that it was Alyssa. She leaned towards me, "This is boring, let's get out of here."

"I need to get this stuff down," I replied in an attempt to stick to my goal of attending all of my classes.

"Listen, I will get you the notes from this girl next to me. She is going to stay. C'mon we'll grab a coffee," Alyssa replied and since she has probably never been told "no" in her whole life, she began packing up without even awaiting an answer from me. I figured I really didn't want to be here anyways, and, if I could just get the notes instead, why not go grab a coffee with a girl who I almost slept with a few nights back? This seems more like my style anyway. I tossed my textbook, course kit, and notebook in my book bag and followed Alyssa out of the lecture hall, trying not to arouse any suspicion from the professor, even though I knew he probably didn't take it personally. We headed past the pillars and down a flight of stairs towards a Starbucks that was located in the student center. We didn't utter a word to each other until after we purchased our five dollar, mocha frappe whatever, and sat down at a small circular table.

"I really thought you would have followed me after we walked in on those two," Alyssa said as she slowly sipped her bubbling, pretentious drink.

"Yeah, I got distracted and then lost you in the crowd, I guess."

"I spent the rest of the night trying to find you. The place got crazy. There was a trail of blood running through the house. All of the stoned people started to think we were in one of those bad teensploitation horror movies," Alyssa said. She let out a soft gentle laugh recalling the stoner hysteria from that night. She was an absolutely beautiful girl. Her short hair perfectly accentuated her face, and she appeared as if she was always hiding a smile but knew a smile is not always well received in this day and age. Her fingers were long and bony, but the rest of her body looked well proportioned and well-rounded. She dressed in vintage and retro clothes, wearing a t-shirt that showed The Clash and sporting spiked wristbands. I couldn't take my eyes off Alyssa, and I hadn't even touched my coffee yet.

"It's good to see you in class, Jack."

"Yeah I know I am rededicating myself to school. I want to go abroad," I replied, all the while sticking to my guns about my epiphany. Remorse about leaving class began to set in, and I realized I had already let myself down. I figured as long as I got those notes my guilt should simply wash away. I glanced at my watch and realized it was close to noon, and I was beginning to get hungry. I really wasn't so into having lunch with other people, so I would have to ditch Alyssa.

"When's your next class?" I asked her.

"At noon. I have Study of Religions, so I actually better head out now. Listen, I would love it if you gave me a call this weekend, and we could hang out."

"Absolutely. I'll call you this Friday," I replied as she wrote her number down on a napkin and handed it to me. I shoved it in my jean pocket and gave her a nod as I left the Starbucks and headed towards the Hound for lunch. It occurred to me that I should come back here later tonight to meet Adam and catch up with him. I didn't see Adam all summer, and as I pondered this, I remembered that when I wasn't working I was merely getting high in my room or in Luke's basement. It was a summer I would rather forget as I was embarrassed by how much money I spent on coke, weed and booze, and how I removed myself from even considering the notion of going out. Many mornings I would wake up with blood on my pillow and a dry throat vowing to never touch the shit again. By at least four in the afternoon I had placed another order.

I was starving and luckily for me The Hound was pretty empty, but still quite loud. The noise was every person speaking loudly plus the sounds of cell phones ringing. Dozens of text messages were sent simultaneously, and I could see people feverishly typing away on their phones, trying to keep the electronic conversations going back and forth. I could hear some conventional conversations bandied around and none of them struck me as relevant, which did not surprise me one bit. As per usual, I inhaled my lunch and left money on the table without asking for the bill.

I decided to head back to my room and relax for a bit. I had this tendency to walk on grass as opposed to cement, a quirk I always failed to explain to myself or to others. I kept my head down and walked along the soft, green grass through clouds of smoke and walls of conversations. Seeing Alyssa again reminded me of Megan and what she had endured. I was never good in dealing with people in the aftermath of their trauma, so avoidance was the way for me to go. I walked past the Student Center and the Computer Engineering Building, up a flight of stairs and across a catwalk towards the biology building. The campus was quite innovative for its time. Enclosed bridges, referred to as catwalks, were built to connect almost all of the buildings together. The catwalks were ingenious and convenient. One never had to step foot outside during the winter months. The traffic was the only negative, as it was usually quite hectic.

As I journeyed through the impressive catwalk, my eyes were so firmly fixed on the ground; I didn't even see her coming. Her head thrust into my left shoulder, and we both fell a few steps back. Her bag fell to the ground, and she scrambled, hoping nobody had seen our carelessness. I shook my head from side to side trying to elude the double vision that was temporarily plaguing me from the impact. The last thing I needed was a concussion. I raised my head for what felt like the first time in awhile, and I gazed at the culprit. She was a little thin girl with relatively long blonde hair. There was no way she could have weighed much more than one hundred pounds and she went up to about my shoulders, which made her quite short. She was wearing a blue tank top and a short little yellow skirt. Her hair went just past her shoulders, and there was a little black clip placed squarely in the dead center of her head. She had big eyes and light freckles scattered around her face. I stared at her, and she kept looking up at me as she repacked her school bag. If I wasn't such a stupid guy, I would have helped her up and gotten her fallen possessions for her, but I wasn't a smart man, and all I could do was stare at her.

"I'm so sorry about that. My head was down. I didn't see you coming," I said as I finally reached down to give her a hand in standing up.

"It's okay. I wasn't paying attention either. Are you okay?" She replied to me in a soft voice with a hint of a Boston accent.

"Yeah, I'm fine, thanks. Do I know you from somewhere?" Okay, I know that I have never seen her before, but there was an attraction there. I had to make some move before she just walked away. Acting like this disgusted me, but I figured in this stage of any relationship its okay to pull a few old-fashioned moves.

"I don't think so, my name is Catherine."

"Jack, Jack Geary. Where are you headed?"

She looked as if she was in some kind of rush as she was constantly looking to both sides of me, refusing to make any form of eye contact. "Just going to Starbucks to do my readings for my classes later today. Normal student shit I guess. What about you?" A smile overcame her formerly straight mouth. She had a presence about her, a sort of charisma. One of those intangible things you look for in people but never truly find.

"I was just going to get a coffee myself."

"Why don't you join me then, Jack? If you're not heading to class or anything," Catherine said.

"Yeah, sure." I figured a third cup of coffee wouldn't kill me. We proceeded back down the path and back to the coffee shop where I had just spent time with Alyssa.

"You're a pretty reckless walker, Jack. I'd hate to see you handle a car," Catherine said as I held the door open for her.

"Yeah, I'm a pretty reckless guy. I try not to live like a hemophiliac in a razor-blade factory." I said trying to give her a chance to laugh at my joke before I did. I was trying my best not to come across as some idiot, trying to pose as Fonzie or James Dean or something. I hope she caught the tone of my speech.

We ordered two cups of coffee, and I took mine and poured some milk in it and we sat down at the same table that Alyssa and I were sitting a mere hour ago. She crossed her legs and placed her hands on the table and looked at me attentively.

"So what do you study?" she asked.

"I'm a history student, you?"

"I'm in Law and Society," Catherine said, and I breathed an enormous sigh of relief. A girl with even a slight amount of ambition was an exciting notion. I was going to ask her if she owned Uggs and wore a thong with sweatpants, but I had just met her.

"I like your accent. You sound kind of like a retarded child." I wish I sometimes thought before I opened my mouth, especially in the hyper-sensitive new millennium. Luckily for me she laughed.

"Wow, so not a Boston fan, I take it?" Catherine replied after she was able to calm her laughter down.

"No, it's a great city; it's beautiful and feels quaint and safe. I love going to school here, but unfortunately I haven't seen much of the city for whatever reason. I must admit I absolutely hate the Red Sox. I mean eighty-six years without a championship, and people start to believe in a curse. It sounds pathetic to me. I mean c'mon a fucking curse. Are you serious?" My anger on this issue was beginning to surface, but she was such a light-hearted person that she found it more entertaining and wasn't getting defensive at all.

"Fair enough, but, hey, Babe Ruth works in mysterious ways," she replied to my tirade.

I began to hang on every word that came off her tongue, and everything she revealed about herself I found exciting and different. She was cut from a different mold than other girls on this vapid campus. Her mannerisms were different than most girls who would just constantly be trying to catch their reflection in any adjacent mirror in the surrounding environment. I began to marvel at her preciousness and the looks she would flash during moments of silence.

"Do you like your roommates?" Catherine asked.

"Yeah, I have been friends with them for a long time, one of them since before high school."

"You're lucky, all of my friends went out of town for school, so I got stuck with a lesbian, some Korean girl, and the poster child for proud anorexics who triumphed over childhood obesity," Catherine said, and I began to admire her candor and how her thought process resembled my own. She had this sweet viciousness to her, which was endearing. She had a way of making everything sound friendly and airy. It was an amazing quality to find in a person. I wish I possessed it.

"Needless to say the four of us are not so close; I haven't even seen the Korean girl since frosh week." Catherine continued on about her living arrangements, confiding in me about the seclusion she feels when she is in her room and how she feels her year would be a lot better if she had roommate which she could relate to. In the past five years, I cannot recall meeting a girl like her, so the chances of her having roommates similar to her seemed quite improbable to me. She felt the same isolation that I felt, the same inner notion that I am not like my friends or other contemporaries who filled the vacuum of my life. We are few and far between, but we are little buried treasures, who will never be discovered lying there feet below the sand. The average person in my generation stands at arm's length from human contact and intimacy; we search for sexual gratification and connect only to modems; but every now and then there is a break in the routine and you meet someone who is different.

"Are you still with me here, Jack?" Catherine asked as she tilted her head, trying to peer into my eyes.

"Yeah, sorry, my mind drifts from time to time. Nothing personal." I said as my voice began to crack. I was truly moved by this chance encounter. If people didn't walk carelessly, we might never fall in love I guess. Weird universe. Love, what an antiquated notion.

"You know what? I think I better get going. I am beat and should crash for a bit. But I would love to go out with you this weekend, if you're free," I said anxiously.

"You got it, Jack. Give me your digits--I'll call you on Friday," she said to me confidently as she saved my number in her cell phone and then put the phone back in her bag. I didn't have a cell so she wrote her number down on a napkin for me. I walked away from her, out of the Starbucks, and towards Drake. This so far had been a fairly productive day. My plan to become a diligent student pretty much went out the window before noon, but I had pleasant encounters with the opposite sex, which should never be discounted.

I finally arrived at my residence room and immediately hopped into bed, jeans on and everything. I felt calm and at peace and that maybe, just maybe I had actually achieved something today.

Chapter 9

I had slept soundly all night as Drake is on the south end of campus, yet I heard through people that ambulances and emergency workers were calming the situation until well into the morning. One student was dead, dozens were injured, and many were arrested, and I slept like a baby all night while the atmosphere of this college had been altered. The ambulances, police, and EMS vacated the school along with the dead, injured, and incarcerated.

News about the incident traveled through the campus like a rash. Every conversation was concerned with this seemingly capricious event. I awoke late and headed out of my room immediately. All I could hear were echoes of the insanity which occurred last night and the consequences of it.

At a late night rally for free speech, as the clock began to move into the early morning, the administration had grown tired of the events occurring on campus. The campus security is essentially useless so the police were called, and violence erupted as students were battered and thrown into paddy wagons. Others were merely handcuffed and placed along the walls. The administration claimed that the rally was disrupting campus life and student living.

The tragedy of the crime occurred when one student, named Randy Tubor, had for some reason, lost his mind and reached for an officer's handgun, which was sleeping in its holster. What he was trying to accomplish is beyond me, but he took it. Randy Tubor was shot in the chest and died immediately amidst all of the chaos.

The rally didn't turn violent until the authorities arrived and up until then it was more hanging out then anything else. I had walked past the area a few times and saw no camaraderie or unity, there was no chanting or speaking of a political agenda of any sort. It was a meek and mild-mannered rally, the likes of which half of the people attending had no clue what the importance of free speech really is, and even if they did they probably would never even exercise that right. It was not worth losing a young life, and the thought of parents having to bury their child cause of an administrations' stupidity is more than upsetting.

A candlelight vigil was to be held later in the day for Tubor and the other victims. I decided not to attend, even though I genuinely felt for him and his loved ones. It was the price to pay for all involved, and he consciously entered into the situation. It's the price of political reform, even if he wasn't an activist. Collateral damage, casualty of war--who gives a fuck? They are all buzzwords for the same no-name asshole that dies in some kind of battle.

It's sad to think of Tubor's body on a cold, metal slab because of a pathetic attempt by a student body to be important, and for a fascist administration to wield its self-proclaimed power.

I stayed on campus all day and watched as young men and women filled the land. They seemed more distant than usual. I sat on a ledge on the aptly named concrete beach, and read the newspaper. I sensed that students weren't preoccupied with attending classes or studying after what occurred in the morning hours. I slept soundly as so many lives were turned upside down. I have no idea what I could have done, but I would have liked to have been there. I flipped through the Boston Globe, and there was no mention of Randy Tubor. Maybe the event happened after the paper was printed, but it would have been nice to see.

I noticed how diverse the campus was, but how we were all sharing the same feelings at the moment. There was some sort of connection in the looks on everyone's faces. Various thoughts filled my head. The thoughts appeared so raw and abstract, and they kept jumping back and forth. I thought of Tubor and about hate in general and the actions that hate can inspire. I grabbed a pen from my inside jacket pocket and on the newspaper I wrote the first passage which was aroused in my mind. If I remember correctly it read,

"I remember. I remember a time when hate was an idea to decipher, not an ideal to consume. We hate without knowing and without care or reprisal. Is it truly inherent to hate, or just convenient? We are at our brightest as children; we never turn a blind eye to anyone; anyone can be an ally. We never refuse to play with someone because of their race, sexual orientation or proclivity, nor because of their political affiliation. We hate commies, homos, blacks, Jews and women for no other reason than it is easier to marginalize than to embrace. We never stop to ask. I wonder if anyone realizes what will be left once the others are marginalized. Probably just a staunch, white, Republican creamy center."

The campus was desolate, it was tangible. The only souls you saw were lifeless and limp as they tried to move on. This incident just didn't have a lasting affect on me as it did many of the other students. It has only been a few days since the Tubor incident, as it would come to be known, yet it felt like a moot point for me. I didn't know him; therefore, I felt it almost impossible for me to care.

I was in one of my moods again. My shoulders felt as if they were cannons ready and willing to fire at anyone. I ran my fingers through my hair and tried my best to alleviate my feeling of worthlessness. When does potential become fulfillment? When do thoughts become the next great book? When do feelings find validation? How can I be plagued with thoughts so self-evident, yet they merely zoom over the heads of others leaving me to do nothing but wonder. Are they self-evident? I am most likely just fooling myself. These questions pounded my stupid brain and created a vacuum within me. I feel empty, not because I am not loved, but because I see nothing to love.

I picked up and dialed. Rejection would not leave me feeling any worse. This feeling could not have been created by Tubor. I just didn't possess that kind of empathy. I know this about myself. The phone rang for what felt like an eternity, until a raspy, yet feminine, voice answered. It was her. It was Catherine. I felt elated, but more importantly I felt something. The conversation was no longer than a few minutes, but I was not in the mood for any banter. She accepted my offer to get a drink at around 8 pm, and I could tell she heard the cracking of my voice and wasn't sure if it was nervousness or delight. I hung up the phone and felt better.

The day passed by. I was excited and wanted the evening to go well. I promised myself I would not present myself as different or as critical or hateful. I was going to be normal. I was going to be who she was looking for. That guy who everyone loves, even though he is like everyone else. Not a prototype but a clone. I saw Luke and Mark in the kitchen as I was getting ready. I knew what they were thinking, and they were utterly wrong. I thought of my past relationships where I either bailed on the girl or got dumped because I fell too hard. These thoughts were filling the caverns of their minds. Why go see movies if they all have the same ending? This idea always crossed my mind when I met a girl I liked, because I felt as if I knew how it would end. Catherine was going to meet me at my room, and I needed to get ready. I heard the knock on the door; I walked as slowly as I could to not give away my excitement. I opened the door, trying to look as casual as possible and there she was.

Chapter 10

We were in love. We fell fast and hard, and it was intense right from the beginning. She constantly matched my wit, and refused to put up with my shit. She was strong and countered every ridiculously negative thought I had. Catherine was a robust girl and was more than my equal in every aspect of life. I loved her. After a few weeks, the loneliness of being away at school had evaporated and I was happy. Plans of running off to Europe to study abroad did not appeal to me anymore. She had this look she threw my way, a lot of time I would just see it out of the corner of my eye. It spoke volumes to me. It was different from the other looks I received from people. It was a look of tranquility and of understanding.

We spent time together almost everyday, whether it was at night or merely in between classes. Catherine allowed me to be myself around her, but by being with her I recognized how problematic my way of thinking was.

I confided in her about how I felt towards the students of this college, and she constantly reassured me that they were not as one-dimensional as I thought. She laughed at many of my observations and told me that I was similar to the people I had written off or marginalized in my mind.

Many weekends, Catherine and I ventured out into Boston and had an amazing time together. We would go to shows, movies, concerts at the Fleet Center or Hatchshell, or sometimes we would just grab a coffee from some street vendor. We explored the city which was home to her but still new to me. I had been here for a year and a half now, but I had rarely left the campus for any reason. Catherine told me about an old movie theatre, where they ran films by Renoir, Berman, and Fellini amongst others. The odd time they even played old cartoons that had been banned from television. Catherine rarely wanted to sit through this type of entertainment, but I dragged her to that theatre many nights to watch whatever was being shown. We walked around Quincy Market and watched the street performers, and then we would take the train to Brookline. We loved the atmosphere of the streets near Fenway, whether a game was going on or not. I was ashamed for not exploring the city more thoroughly until I met Catherine.

One weekend she even brought me to her home in Springfield to meet her parents. Her father was an investment banker and her mother a paralegal. They were both more than decent people and reminded me very little of my own parents, which I could never decide if I felt this was a good or bad thing. They were always kind and generous to me and I didn't know if it was because they liked me or they just wanted to see Catherine remain happy. The house she grew up in suited me perfectly; it was cozy as it sat nestled between to postmodern eyesores. As a structure it paled in comparison size-wise to the neighboring homes. It was quaint and perfect and even had a white picket fence that separated it from the sidewalk. I truly loved it. Her house seemed like it stood for a long forgotten ideal to me, I can't fully explain it. After visiting her neighborhood, my home in Seattle felt even further away.

I felt different with her and I had grown excited about being away at college for the first time since I had arrived. The campus felt different to me, and the people who I had developed a disdain for in my first year, now looked fresh in my eyes. It was all Catherine's doing and because of her I had even made some more friends. My roommates even noticed a change in my disposition, even though I was still using drugs for recreation.

I stayed in her room and I would only return home to see my roommates or to take some hits of coke. The only thing Catherine couldn't help me with was my lingering habits. I still smoked and indulged in coke whenever I could. This was all to her dismay, but I simply enjoyed them too much. She had been a wonderful influence and I could honestly say at that point I thought I was happy. I no longer looked for the flaws in the student body, and I saw them as capable human beings. She had erased so many feelings that I had adhered to since High School. She was wonderful in almost every way, and the sex was incredible. We were both very in tune with one another during the process, knowing every peak and valley of each other's bodies while flowing in and out of the sheets and on and off the mattress with reckless abandon.

At times, when we were together I felt so different, that it scared me. For some odd reason I had grown accustomed to whom I had become. Even though I was more likeable now, it was startling for me to have shifted my personality so drastically. I had become happy in my solitude and the things I thought and felt were genuine. I had many negative thoughts since I had come to this campus, but they were real and they belonged to me. I could not understand what was wrong with me. Catherine made me a better person, but I just could not accept that that better person as who I really was.

Months had passed since Catherine and I had bumped into each other's lives. It was a rough transition at first from being single and free to being dependent and part of something. The feeling ate away at me sometimes that this was my new life. As much as I loved her, the feelings began to dissolve my core. I was becoming stifled and gagged, and I felt as if the inevitable moment when I was to hurt her would feel like the universe was out of sync. When we first got together, my universe felt right. I tried to distance myself from her because the thought of dropping the hammer on her was excruciating. She was too perceptive to not realize it or to merely shrug it off.

When I saw her, she looked angelic amongst a backdrop of noise emanating from other rooms in the building. As we sat on her bed, I knew our relationship was coming to an end. I had been meaning to end it for some weeks now but it was too difficult. Finally, I looked at her and saw the look in her eye. She knew what was coming. I began to burst with emotions as she grabbed me and placed my face onto her shoulder. Her shirt filled with tears as I let loose. I knew it was breaking her heart just to watch me. I had to get out before the walls officially closed in on me. My vision became foggy and misty, and the taste of salt filled my mouth. I got up and left her living room. I opened the door and slammed it shut; there was no way for me to be subtle now. I haven't felt like this in so long, especially when I considered how happy I was over winter break when we were together. I had become completely unhinged.

As I walked away from the door, I could hear the chain-lock being placed on the latch. This felt like closure, but I knew it didn't sit right with me. I frantically turned around and approached the door. It seemed as if it was made of titanium and without hinges and would never open for me again. I stood there. I would not be able to permeate the door but a voice did make its way through.

"Just leave." Catherine said as her voice began to crack.

"I will, but, Catherine, I'm sorry," I yelled through the door.

"Why won't you let me be with you? Why are you scared of being happy? You are so stubborn, it's almost as if you don't want to be happy because you think it is trendy. I hate you sometimes," said Catherine.

I lost it and pounded my trembling fist on the door. I wanted her to take that comment back or at least to not say it with such conviction. The word hate pierced my ears, flowed through my brain, and came pouring out of my eyes. I hate this shit.

"Over time you will realize that falling in love with me was the worst decision you have ever made. I'm sorry." I yelled to her over the great, titanium divide which was separating us. That door was me, and I was that door. I stopped yelling and began to listen. The hall was silent and for a brief second I could actually just hear the Earth rotating peacefully. I put my hand on the door, and I could sense she was still there with her back to the door. I could feel the pumping of her chest and her hand covering her eyes. I didn't know if she could sense if I was still there. I already missed her, and I knew that tomorrow this feeling of despair would grow to be something even more dreadful.

I left the hallways and could see a few people peeking out of their rooms to see what the commotion was. People would watch car wrecks all day, if the person behind didn't honk their horns. I stood outside of her dorm and attempted to peer through her window. I could only see the darkness and the flickering of television stations. I stood there wondering if what I just did would amount to one of the biggest regrets of my life. I knew that I gave up on her too early, but I had to be selfish.

I stood there amongst the snow and pollution, under the moonlight, remembering that it was not always good times between Catherine and me. This was important to focus on as well. She grew tiresome of my exploits and the uncertainty which comes with my emotions. I tried to curb my cocaine use to only weekends, which to her was two times a week too many. She was very driven and ambitious, whereas I deemed my own ambition to be wishful thinking. I guess the good met evenly in the middle with the bad, but it was not enough to keep me satisfied. I never fully trusted her either and I knew she judged me in between flailing moments of falling in love. I never told her about my relationship with the priest for that exact reason.

I had gone to see him only once in the past few months, after being on a steady diet of conversations with him throughout most of first semester. The priest and I would meet, and we never even mentioned religion for the most part. Our relationship had grown to become more than a theological debate by two men on opposite sides of the fence, who were unwilling to peek over. The fence had morphed into some kind of makeshift bridge, which allowed us to experience one another's perspectives no matter how much we hated them. He understood me, and I tried my best to understand why he took such a liking to me. Was I his little salvation project? If I saw the light, would I be his golden ticket to walk in the kingdom of heaven? I don't know. It could be that he just liked my take on things. Maybe we really do like people who are not similar to us. We hear them speak, we hate what they have to say, and it gives us validation for our thoughts and beliefs.

There was no way she was going to peek through the window now; she would never think I would just stand outside for this amount of time. I flipped the collar of my jacket up and walked away. I knew that even on a campus of fifty thousand students, plus faculty and support staff, that we would run into each other at some point. Her head would crash into my chest, and we would have the chance to fall in love all over again. To feel what we originally felt. Does love ever dissolve to the point where the feelings can never arise again? I had no idea, but based on my past experiences, love does not always resurface and when it does it is usually for carnal reasons. A glimmer of hope and nothing more, I suppose.

Fuck. I really hate this shit. I hoped Catherine would realize that I was a mistake and a week later I would see her grinding with some guy at some random dirty little club. I deserved it; I fully deserved any future hurt that was sent my way with her return address on it.

I finally arrived back at Drake, but upon reaching the door I failed to hear the dangling of any keys in my pockets. I placed my head against the door and didn't even see a light on inside. I knocked persistently and began to grow infuriated that no one cared enough to roll out of their hangovers to let me in from out of the snowfall. I would kill to be in my bed right now and to let this day mercifully end. I finally gave up on my peers caring about me outside in the cold, and I headed back towards the main part of campus.

I figured I could head back to Catherine's to sleep. She was compassionate enough to at least let me crash on her couch, but I was too proud for that. I could probably head to the church, it was always open. He might even be there, but I think that a few people (most likely homeless) would probably be crashing there already. I didn't feel like having company tonight anyways. I had no money for a hotel or motel. Hell, I didn't even have a quarter to use a pay phone to call student services to come open my door. Desperation began to sink in, as I wondered where I would spend the night. I felt like punching myself in the face for having been so stupid as to forget my keys.

The snow began falling heavily on to the ground and limited my visibility to only a few feet in front of me. Whenever I heard a noise, I turned around hoping it was someone on their way to a warm place and that I could tag along. The wind picked up and held me back as I tried to force my way through it. I could hear the whistling of the wind as it pushed me back inches at a time. Finally, I gave up my resistance against nature and succumbed to its persuasion. I fell and landed flat on my back. The ground was frozen and so cold that it made me instantly tear. I could barely move, so I lay there and just stared into the ether of the winter night and shivered. Where would I even go at this time of the night? I rolled unto my front and lifted myself to my feet as quickly as I could. I stood up and continued battling the elements in an attempt to find shelter.

I came to the realization that the church would be the only place open at this time of the night. I walked diligently in its direction and could even see it from afar. I felt like the faster I walked towards it, the more distant it appeared. The sensation of never reaching it burdened me, and it became the only place in the world I wanted to be right then. Maybe that was its deceptive allure to all outsiders. It was what many would give their lives for but could never enter its sacred walls. It was an oasis in the desert, an illusion which encompassed the sanctity of one single, original thought, which spurred a movement of billions. Yet, the question remains: how do we reach its gates?

The holy building and I must have met somewhere in the middle, because I finally reached its inviting doors. I made my way down my usual path, up the stairs, straight into the vast cathedral, and sat down in my usual spot. I began to think how this place made me think of cigarettes. My willpower is roughly that of a six-year-old child, so I proceeded to light a cigarette. I supposed I could just sleep on one of the pews. If there was a desert nearby, I probably would pull a St. Antony and live alone in the desert but right now I am just out of luck.

I gazed upon the high ceilings and stain glass depictions of the passion. I arched the upper half of my body, leaned forward, and placed my elbows on my knees. I could hear stirring in a room adjacent to where I was sitting. When I was a child, before the death of my father, it was nearly impossible to get me in a place like this. He was not much of a religious man or a man of immense conviction; it was usually my mother who gave us even a semblance of faith. As I grew up, I despised the church as I began to understand its pervasive influence in my world. I don't like the idea of being strangled, and I don't get off on institutional asphyxiation. This had been a horrible night so far, and I had known it was going to be.

Suddenly a voice emerged from behind a tied up curtain.

"Kind of late, isn't it?"

"Hey, I locked myself out. In this weather, I didn't know where else to go," I replied to the priest who loomed over me. The priest sat down about a foot away from me on the same pew. He looked tired and weary and not at all surprised by my visit. "How come you are here so late?" I asked him.

"I sleep at the church; I have an apartment in the back there. I usually don't sleep much anyways. Why do you keep coming back here? You genuinely hate this place, Jack."

"I don't know. Tonight, I had no other option. It's quiet as well, which I appreciate, but I honestly don't know."

"You are not the first person to not understand why they are drawn here. I guess that is the purpose of faith. I remember many a time at a church where I worked in Philadelphia; we had many people in the community openly wondering why they entered through our front doors. People lose faith, and this is a place where it can be restored."

I didn't want to tell the priest that the notion that he just presented to me only pushed me further away from this place.

"I ended it with Catherine tonight."

He paused for a brief second.

"I knew it was only a matter of time for you. Don't you ever worry that you are becoming the things you hate in other people?" the priest said to me in a very solemn tone.

"Not at all. That's ridiculous," I replied back to him. The things I hate in people are materialism and apathy; I hate those corporate or selfish assholes. I had not become them at all.

"You hurt someone for no other reason than you didn't want to admit you were happy because, if you're happy, you might forget how much fun you have hating everyone else. If you don't hate them, then you just won't be you. You fear you will be like them. Blissful and ignorant."

"I want to be happy, even in a good relationship how I could be happy in this piece of shit world? How could I be happy in a world where we fight bullshit wars, where SUV's are more celebrated than literature and where a tool like the Internet is not used for freedom of speech or to collapse geography but for the purpose of downloading porn?" My voice was beginning to slip as my anger grew. I wanted to be happy. I knew this about me. I was not scared to be happy; I didn't need to listen to this bullshit.

"Jack, finding one person who understands you makes this world tolerable. It makes living in a world that lacks morals almost worthwhile."

"How come the church frowns on homosexuality? If you find that person and they happen to be of the same sex, why does that not make this world easier to endure?"

"I have no problem with homosexuality. A few students who are part of my congregation are gay."

"So what? You are some kind of radical, hippie priest, is that it?"

The priest and I both found my assessment amusing; he had considerable trouble keeping his laughter in. I just could not understand him, no matter how hard I tried. He barely followed Catholic dogma, yet he believed in the same fundamental beliefs. It truly baffled me. If he was ever invited to ecumenical councils, he would probably have to sit on the left side all alone.

"You must feel so protected within these walls. I mean you are not even really allowed to have true and diverse relationships." This comment ended all the residual laughter that had just begun to fill the hollow church.

"I have had relationships in my life. I have lost a lot. I have yet to regret entering into this line of work. Maybe it has made me more distant from people, but I have lost enough up to that point." The priest looked over at me and hunched his body.

"What have you lost?" I asked him without contemplation.

"Well, my father died when I was a young man just like you, and my wife died after twenty-five years of marriage. I have tried at life and failed like many do. I needed a place where I would not be confronted with those situations again. I know it's not right, and I do not preach my choice to others. To you it seems cowardly, but it was my choice. I know you can appreciate it, Jack."

"How did your wife die?" I asked. I was finally beginning to connect to something that had to do with religion. The priest lifted his head up with swiftness not usual for someone in their early sixties. He looked at me with a piercing look much like a mother would at a disturbed child.

"She worked at a high school in Philadelphia. We were both teachers there, actually. She loved to teach. She had such a kindness and willingness to deal with being underappreciated."

He paused for another second before continuing.

"One day, some asshole student opened fire on the cafeteria and a stray bullet caught her in the chest. The student then turned the gun on himself. That was it. This was long before Columbine. It wasn't a tense time for teachers in the media yet. Twenty-five years gone to shit, Jack," the priest said as if he had told the story a thousand times but not in many years.

"Holy fuck. I don't even know what to say." For the first time in all of our conversations, I actually felt as if the priest was not a worker for the church, but someone who had nowhere else to turn to.

"Anyways, that was years ago. Here, Jack. Come to my apartment. You can sleep on my couch. It is getting late."

That night that the priest let me stay at his place, I learned a lot about him. He told me in detail how he ended up in this situation. He told me all about his wife, his old job and life. He explained to me what his life had become, and about the daily routine he was comfortably nestled into. After I left his house the next morning, I researched on the internet what he had told me even further and uncovered the whole story. I found out everything about what happened to his wife. For a brief moment, his life was an actual headline. Between what the priest told me and what I found on my own, I felt as if I knew everything about this man.

After he went to bed, I had trouble falling asleep so I decided to look around his apartment, to see what else I could uncover about him. I know I was being invasive, but I was in a mischievous mood and he had intrigued me. His apartment was small, even for the standards rendered by traditional Christianity. He had little to no space to eat, relax, or even think. The kitchen merged into the living room, and the chair given to him was to be used for both eating and watching television. The walls were a dark grey hue and made the room feel smaller than it actually was. Either way, it was a small environment, and no pastel color could change that.

I was completely disgusted by the kitchen. How could anyone ask a man to prepare his meals in this area? There was an old toaster oven and what appeared to be the first household electric stove. The grey walls near the stove had oil splatter on them, and I had assumed that the priest did not care to have them cleaned. I opened a few cupboards and saw nothing but a couple boxes of crackers, baking soda and rice. I always figured that he was a minimalist by personality and trade. The more I looked around his kitchen the more I felt that it uncovered aspects of who he was.

After I experienced his living conditions, I assumed that the priest was a man devoid of any creativity. He had very few books or paintings or any form of artistic expression in his home. He was a symbol of how the world is the cancer to idealism. I felt that he had become a reluctant creature of habit, but nonetheless habit ruled his day-to-day life. He told me how he would awaken each morning and he would sit in bed and place his glasses on his rotund face. He had hours until he was required to be at the church, in the off-chance that a student needed some spiritual guidance.

I saw pictures of his wife and she was not a stunning woman by any stretch of the imagination. He told me that he simply adored her and longed for her the minute they locked eyes at a downtown bookstore in Philadelphia. He was a young-looking twenty-six-year old and she was a twenty-one-year old who appeared as if she had just been let out of Sunday school. Her ankle length, tight skirt revealed as little as her wayward smirk did. He could tell she was uneasy about being an object of desire, as he stared at her; she did her best to avoid his glare. Her attempts to avoid him were futile, as he finally approached her surprisingly easily penetrable cocoon.

He described how he loved her long, stick straight hair, her firm body, and her unwillingness to give up on his always changing moods. She was tall, thin, and dressed as if she rarely left the house. The priest often accused her of being uni-polar and out of touch with the world. He was gravely mistaken though, and he mistook her positive outlook as an aversion to the truth. He would constantly mull over the trite daily musings and trivial horrors that he would come across in the newspaper, yet everything that occurred outside the walls of their apartment was of no use to her. She possessed the ability to calm him down no matter what transpired outside of their decorated one bedroom cube.

The priest told me that everyone was surprised to hear that he and Sara were married. The two of them, were both extremely quiet and even a bit awkward around other faculty members. She taught English and was mesmerizing at making students fall in love with Lee, Shakespeare, and Orwell. They both adored the written word, yet he focused on history and philosophy as the two disciplines he would try to convey to the cinder blocks posing as students.

While telling his story, he finally brought up the name Chris Zola. To this day he vividly remembers his beloved wife speaking of his untapped potential. He recalls her saying he was a very logical young man and a wonderful essayist. He understood the literature that he was forced to read. In fact, he more than understood it. He mastered every word within it.

The articles and news reports I found later on about Chris Zola and the entire incident, all stated how no one suspected that he fantasized about such morbid events. The research was very detailed on how Zola had become adept at building pipe bombs out of household items and chemicals. He not only created them but he planned on using them. In his room, locked away from his oblivious, sugar-coated parents, he would read books to decipher the world, and it provided solutions for how he could ease his heartbreaking anger. He easily found resources that were willing to show Zola the light and methods to achieve his vengeance. When his retinas finally burned from staring at mountains of information for too long and he was forced to shut down, his reality set in. He was alone. He was alone, angry and scared.

Every article I found made it seem as if Zola didn't have a friend in the world. The only time it appeared that people cared to know that he existed, was to verbally or physically abuse him. He would come home from school with welts on his body and tears welled up in the corner of his eyes. His parents tried to comfort him and told him to try harder to fit in. They reasoned that getting picked on was his doing.

Police reports said they found Zola's journal, which stated that his original desire was to blow up the school. This delusion of grandeur became secondary when he realized how little satisfaction he would derive from it. He wanted to stretch the moment out, to marinate in his joy of staring into the eyes of his contemporaries as they pleaded for life. Zola would become the sustainer of life;

he could end it on a mere whim or force them to thank him everyday for the rest of their lives for granting them continuance. It was so poetic in its simplicity, and Zola loved to retreat to his plan.

Stealing his father's gun was reportedly no obstacle. Bringing it inside his high school was simple (as Zola was a student long before the implementation of metal detectors in public schools), and working up the courage to go through with his desire required no hesitation whatsoever. Zola reached into his pants pocket and pulled out his father's handgun. He pointed it towards the ceiling of the spacious cafeteria. He squeezed the trigger and fired one round into the stale air. Finally, for the first time in his life, Chris Zola was known to the student body. Three bullets exited his father's gun in a cloud of smoke. Screams and fear hurled around the cafeteria for minutes that felt like hours. The sound pierced and electrified the room. Students huddled together and yelled in terror through streams of tears. Zola trembled from power, he loved being in control of the pathetic people who never accepted him, who never allowed him entrance into their stupid little cliques or treated him as nothing more than a waste of sperm.

He squeezed the trigger with aplomb. Where the bullet finished its journey was of no consequence to him. He wanted them all dead, for crimson rivers to flow through the halls of his high school. The teachers who deemed him a failure were no different than the teenagers who wouldn't be his friend. Many years later a report out of a New York newspaper wrote, how Chris Zola never read Catcher in the Rye, he never watched violent films, nor did he enjoy the artificial pleasure of any video game.

He was alone and just wanted someone to see him, a glance, just to be noticed, to not be invisible anymore. He was sick of celebrating his isolation by escaping into his cathartic, nihilistic fantasies.

I felt as if Zola never had anything against the priest's wife. In fact, from what the priest told me in corroboration with news reports, she was the only soul who didn't repulse him or cause him to cry at night. Unfortunately a stray bullet tore through her flowery blouse, then pierced her milky, delicate skin, and finally stormed through her ribcage and put a stop to two hearts at one time. The priest wasn't able to retreat from under the lunch table to help his dying wife. All he could do was watch from afar as her outstretched arm extended towards him.

Chris Zola reserved the last bullet for his anger-riddled brain and when he had seen enough blood splatter on the walls, he arched his arm, placed the barrel firmly on his temple and began his entry into restful peace he had dearly hoped was awaiting. His limp, pleased body fell to the floor. One news report out of Philadelphia stated, that just prior to the final bullet being fired one could see a smile on Zola's face, for the first time while he was inside the walls of the place he hated more than anything.

From the moment I set foot inside his church and opened my mouth to allow my confusion to pour out, the priest told me he was reminded of another young man who was dead now. He saw me and saw a young man toiling away in his room late at night, dreaming of killing his peers and wishing someone would understand him. The priest knew that I would probably never open fire on the unsuspecting campus, but he knew it wasn't about that.

I remember the priest beginning to get emotional as he spoke to me about his morning routine. The priest's mornings were filled with a flood of unwanted memories. Images of his wife getting ready in the morning would become so intense that he could project it into reality. He would lie in bed and not move until something aroused him to. He would stare at his wife as she would go through the motions of her morning. She would stand in their room as if she still existed, as if she had called in sick that day. Sara was standing there, and as always trying in vain to awaken her husband from his hibernation.

"Robert, Robert." He could still hear the voice echoing throughout his dreams. Her death made him wish that they had had children. Sara told him that she wasn't able to bear children on their second date, as if knowing that he was the one she would marry. He envisioned them adopting but the wait was longer than she had to give. Every moment of everyday, he questioned his rushed decision to be ordained. It was a rush decision for what would be a long process, but maybe he was ordained because he was the only person willing to work at the local college campus. He knew he was destined to be a shepherd without a flock, and that suited him to a tee. Much like me, he had a disdain for the campus and its inhabitants. I felt that only out of fear of becoming a pillar of salt prevented him from turning his back on those who never even entered the church. He was not a religious man, even after his wife was taken from him, but he was a man whose body had filled to the brim with such numbness that he saw no other option. After the funeral and after the condolences stopped coming in, he was alone. As a man who rested heavily on fate, he grew increasingly worried about meeting another Sara.

Photographs of the priest on the wall of his apartment, showed the priest as a slender man with a full head of hair. Not even a single wrinkle was visible on his face. Years later his waist expanded, his hair thinned and no one called or visited the former teacher. His only brother got sick of speaking to an answering machine, and his friends knew that any invitation would go unrewarded. This was how the priest wanted it to be, for without Sara there was no intimacy in the world, no connection and no underlying point. The flow of his world had flatlined.

I appreciated how open the priest was in opening up that night in his apartment. He showed me a facet of himself, that I could never had imagined existed. He opened a window for me to leer into, and see how he became the man that I knew. The details he conveyed about his emotions and actions, made him even more endearing.

I woke up bright and early the next morning on a baby blue suede couch, which if I had been in alive in the '70's would have made me somewhat nostalgic. I was exhausted as the priest and I had stayed up talking after entering his home. I didn't want to wake the priest, so I got dressed quickly and headed out the door. I was going to leave a note, but I figured he would have just assumed that I was thankful. It must have been close to nine by now, and I am sure I could get into my dorm with little to no problem whatsoever.

I walked quickly through the dispassionate and quiet campus, and I couldn't help but think of what the priest had told me the night before. The whole time I had just pictured him being raised in a God-fearing house where he embraced Christianity and waited for the day when the institution would simply embrace him back. In between the church and my dorm was the vigil for Randy Tubor, a cross stuck between two concrete slabs of sidewalk and dozens of bouquets of flowers surrounding it. Rolled up pieces of paper with heartfelt notes littered the cross as well. I wondered how many of those notes were actually written by people who truly loved him. I even contemplated opening a few of them up and reading the messages. This thought passed quickly as it didn't interest me so much.

I walked past the same area I had the night before, but the weather was considerably better. Last night was a revelation for me. Between the experience with Catherine and the priest, I felt weird and different. I had hurt Catherine yet gotten closer to the priest. If anything, I would have thought I would have wanted it the other way around. I really just wanted to go home and relax. In fact, I needed it.

I finally made my way to Drake and was able to grab a closing door just as a girl was walking through it on her way out. Without hesitation, I ran upstairs and opened the door to my room. Luke and Mark were sitting on our couch. Mark was enamored with whatever he was watching, and Luke looked completely baked on whatever he was on. I only hope Luke was still high from the night before and didn't get high this early in the morning. Not like he had classes to worry about, I suppose.

"Where have you been? Feels like I haven't seen you in days, Jack," Luke said when he finally noticed I had entered our common room.

"I got locked out last night, so I stayed at a friend's place."

"Why didn't you just stay at Catherine's?" Luke said, fully knowing we had either broken up or were fighting.

"We ended it last night. Long story I'll save for another time. I don't really feel like discussing it."

"Fair enough, man," Mark chimed into the conversation.

"Luke, can I grab a line from you? I need it," I asked Luke in my most groveling and hyper expression of needing some form of narcotic.

"Of course, here just help yourself. Got a bowl here for you as well if you want."

"Nah, this will do," I said as I sat down on the couch and grabbed the CD case with a slender little line on it just for me. I grabbed the dollar bill and placed in just within my nostril. I inhaled it all. I didn't want to leave a crumb of it on the case when it could have been making its way through my system, alleviating any ill feelings I had. My brain felt less fried and even my hair felt lighter. I absolutely loved this moment, and, even though I knew how dangerous the drug was, this moment made the nose bleeds and heart palpitations almost worthwhile. It's not hard to see why drugs are so appealing and transcend most ethnic groups and age ranges. It does not discriminate against who it will make feel better, and that, I think, is its inherent beauty. It is not even the least subjective; it is who we want to be. We all want to be non-judgmental and have the ability to make people's problems go away.

"Anyone call for me last night?" I asked Mark and Luke.

"I was up all night, and I didn't even hear the phone ring." Mark replied to me.

I don't know why I even thought that Catherine would call, but I had to check just in case I was wrong.

"You alright, Jack, about the Catherine thing?" asked Mark.

"I'll be okay. Where's Peter? I asked trying to switch topics as smoothly as humanly possible.

"He had an 8:30 lecture, should be back afterwards. Jack you should get some more sleep, you look like hell."

"So does Luke," I replied and turned my head to Luke to see if he was going to possibly pass out of consciousness. His hair was as neat as I had ever seen it, but his face looked as if it was having trouble clinging to the bones underneath. Mark always looked fairly well kept, and gave the impression that his mom had some hand in getting him ready every morning. Luke still hadn't responded to my comment about his current appearance. He was completely glazed over and fixated on what was occurring on the television screen even though I doubt it was registering.

I took another line and followed that with another. I knew the next few days would be hazy. I was going to indulge my temptations. Maybe I would even do a little writing. I had always wanted to sit down and write a novel of some sort, maybe this would be the opportune time to take up that endeavor. See what happens, I guess.

Chapter 11

The next three days were spent with a dollar bill lodged firmly up my nostril, which in fact was beginning to ache constantly. I would wake up mid day and immediately reached for a CD case, dollar bill, and my little wrapped up piece of tinfoil. I hated myself for not being able to say no to my weaknesses. I hated myself for not having any ability whatsoever to pour grace on myself. I knew I would eventually kick all of my habits, but these binges constantly startled me.

I began hitting lines at around 1 pm and did so until well into the morning. I sat alone in my room, staring at my computer screen waiting for inspiration to strike like a thief in the night. I finally decided to attempt to go to sleep. I lay down and fell in and out of sleep. My arm rested peacefully under my pillow, which I had my head placed on. I had the TV on, playing on relatively low volume. Every time I fell into my long needed sleep,

I would jump up thinking I was either having a heart attack because my left arm was numb or a stroke because I thought I couldn't hear the TV. It was a horrible night. It was awful to think that if you fell asleep it would be the last time you would be alive.

No symptom that I experienced was bad enough at the time to make me quit or even take a day off. My new cigarettes and coke diet made me feel as if I was playing a daily game of Russian roulette. A losing endeavor no matter how you play it. I would feel amazing at one moment and once that feeling subsided I could get it back so easily. This thought gave me immense comfort, and that comfort was priceless. If I had just one heart attack, I knew it would have been motivation enough to quit.

The allure of coke or getting high in general was easy to decipher. No matter how hard it was to coax myself to try and write my novel or no matter how much I failed at school, I could always succeed at getting high. It was a beautiful process, to begin with a goal in mind and to be successful. It was a success anyone could feel while the rest of their life was littered with failures.

I received neither a call nor an instant message from Catherine during my self-incarceration. She must have known what I was up to and how irresponsible my addictive personality was. As these thoughts went to war against logic in my mind, I scanned the landscape of my room. I hadn't looked at my room in days; my eyes were constantly fixed on the glare of the computer screen or my face was buried in a pillow. It was a tiny cubicle, which looked even smaller because of all of my possessions scattered around the room. Used tissues were piled up, dirty clothes were lying on the floor, and CDs and DVDs were covering every inch of my twin bed. I was a mess. There was no way around it in my own personal assessment. I was fazed but not undone just yet.

I took another line, a thick and monstrous line. It was not coarse at all, and it made my eyes hurt from my pupils being so fixed and alert. I had to remember to blink, or they would become increasingly irritated and dry. I hadn't seen Catherine or the priest for days nor had I attended any classes. I had ditched my plans for a semester abroad, and I began to entertain thoughts of going home and seeing my mom and stepfather. I needed to think this through because I had not left on the best terms. I decided to give it more time and thought. Fuck, I needed to get out of this building.

Chapter 12

My roommates entered and exited my room at will, knowing full well that I was only physically there. There was a look of worry on their faces, but they have been through this with me before. In Luke's case, I had been there for him when his addictions got the best of his sensibility. Peter was annoyed at my behavior, and he was growing weary of my constant relapses into stupidity. I wanted to shake the malaise, but I would look out my window and see the same old shit that goaded me into this precarious situation in the first place. As I peered out of my window from the thirteenth floor of the Drake, past many of the lecture halls and student buildings, I saw a field that was always vacant of people. In this field, whose grass consistently went uncared for, stood a hydro tower that was sandwiched (roughly one hundred feet on each side) by two enormous trees that were brimming with life. I put my computer chair right up to the window and stared at it for hours on end while I indulged. The dichotomy drove me insane at times.

Even the smells would eek through the opening of my window and make their way to my nose and cause an awful olfactory sensation in my brain. Everything on the other side of my far wall was unappealing to who I had become in the past few days.

The smells emanating from outside had begun to fill my room over time. I could smell everything individually; dandelions, fast food, colognes, perfumes, smoke and even the smell of campus commerce broke through the barrier and suffocated me. It was overwhelming and broke the monotony of the past few days. It even had the audacity to provoked memories I had forgotten about or tried hard to suppress; the memories of Catherine, memories of my freshman year or even that of the priest. I shook my head vigorously and rubbed my eyes until they felt inflated and puffy.

I stood up, and my weakened body rushed to the bathroom. I stood in front of the mirror and saw how pale I had become and how unruly my hair was. I took off my clothes and tried to wash the apathy out of my muscles. The shower was brisk and useful, and, as soon as I was dressed, I ran outside, threw the ancient door open, and stood in the unadulterated sunlight. I knelt down and looked up and could see Mark peering through the window of the common room, the look on his face begged to know what was wrong with me. I was smiling for the first time in days. Smell provokes the memory with more ease than any other sense, and it had done the trick for me. I felt gratitude as I stood back up. Even though I had only been out of commission for a few days, I felt renewed. Every threadlike ounce of light that entered my eyes was miraculous, and every scent was a reawakening.

The blur of people rampaged in and out of my field of vision, and I didn't even bother to dissect the emptiness of their actions. It lay dormant in the back of my mind, and I would not dare awake that sleeping giant. I felt as if this binge had ceased. What the priest told me about his past was still a weight on my shoulders. I felt for him more than I felt for my own situation. He lost his wife, his profession, and his life because of one lost soul who got his hand on a gun. He should have done missionary work in Bolivia, instead of coming to this college, if he really wanted to leave his old life behind. He had a sense of his own personal agency, and I admired that. He changed the course of his history whether it was for the right reasons or not. I could not pry anymore into his personal life though. I already felt I had been too invasive.

"Jack, what the fuck are you doing?" yelled Mark from the window above.

"Getting some fresh air. What's the problem?"

"You're acting weird. Come back when you're normal," Mark said through hints of laughter before shutting the window. I enjoyed his comment although I knew his request (in how he meant it) would go unfulfilled. I was normal. There were others like me. I refused to believe otherwise. I began to walk without purpose, yet with defiant conviction. I had no agenda, nowhere to be, and nothing to do. I continued on my pilgrimage to cleanse my body of cocaine, cigarettes, and a failed novel, which I didn't care if it ever got completed. It was a tedious effort.

I walked by what felt like every inhabitant of the campus, and continued right past a full house at The Hound. I glanced at it without slowing down, and I could see a diminutive Adam socializing with other students. This pleased me. The Student Center was packed as well, and I had no intentions of stopping anywhere. I pondered my future without worry and realized I would be put on academic probation once this year was complete, based on the fact that I was probably failing two of my four courses. And again, I was not flustered, worried, or bothered. I felt almost bohemian in my demeanor and current thought process. I jaunted past the Tubor memorial and saw that the flowers had wilted and most of the notes left in his memory had been blown away. I supposed I accomplished what I needed to in my first year and a half of college. Academically I blew it, but I had experienced what I needed for the time being. I, Jack Geary, was not a failure as of this point in time. Not yet.

Chapter 13

If my life was a book would the spine ever get bent? A question with no answer, and yet I searched for one. I doubted it. I had been walking for at least twenty minutes toward an area of campus I had only seldom seen or visited. The buildings were all new and smelled of fresh concrete and the sweat of hard labor. There was construction still proceeding on the exteriors, it was loud and obnoxious. The workers took no notice of the people who passed by, even though these people noticed them. The men appeared as if they had been ripped out of an Upton Sinclair novel. Ragged, dirty and utterly lacking refinement, they oozed ruggedness and a violent sexuality that was apparent at first glance. I gazed at them through a lens of heterosexuality, wondering why I was not like them. This was a day though that I would not allow to be wrecked by any sense of self-doubt.

I stood there motionless as my field of vision became full of bodies in motion and speech bouncing off anything it possibly could. The sun skated across the sky, as its rays became localized in the area of campus I was settled in. The brightness filled the area, and people around me began to remove their sweaters or jackets. I removed my jacket and tucked it under my arm. I tugged at my collar in a desperate attempt to let the breeze flow through my shirt and brush up against my body. The construction workers took a break to let the heat pass. I couldn't blame them. It was suddenly scorching out and the heat from the ground was going through my shoes. I could feel it on my feet.

I couldn't stand the heat bearing down on me anymore, so I began walking towards the part of campus I am more familiar with. My day lacked purpose, and I was falling in love with how it was unfolding. I had a coffee while reading the newspaper at a fair trade coffee shop. Not in opposition to anything, there was just never a lineup at the fair trade stands. Then I perused the campus bookstore. This was a passion of mine that had gone neglected for far too long. I flipped through everything from *The Mandarins* to *The Alchemist* and even a Readers' Digest version of the work of Chomsky. Not all of it appealed to me, but I still wished I didn't sniff all my money away or I would have bought a few.

I left the bookstore empty handed and headed back towards Drake. I walked as slow as possible, still carrying my jacket tucked firmly under my arm. I walked past numerous boutiques selling useless items which students with disposable income just eat up at impulse. Representatives from MasterCard, Visa, and other credit places lined up in the student center to attract students to live beyond their means. It sickened me to watch these assholes try and exploit students and attract them to live in debt. I don't know why I let these things bother me; the world has succumbed to powers greater than the collective will of the good. Most seem to have accepted if not embraced it, but I let it wreck my entire day. I caught the eye of the MasterCard representative, and he seemed sheepish because of his remedial occupation. The added irony of having to do this job on campus at a university must only pour salt on their professional wounds. I have to get out of the student centre before I vomit.

The campus was rowdy and jubilant, and the student body acted as if they were already accomplished, not just privileged. I went against my common sense and entered the campus bar aptly named The Crowd. I felt alone when it seemed everyone else had come in a herd of some sort. I sat down on a stool right in front of the bar and immediately ordered a beer. I nursed it for minutes as I scanned the crowd. I noticed Adam for the second time, sitting in a booth across the bar. It looked as if he was perched up on something. I knew he was short, but there was no way he was sitting on a phonebook or something.

I grabbed my beer and made my way through the crowd. I turned sideways to squeeze by, as no amount of "excuse me" would have been heard. I rubbed up against so many people I almost became embarrassed by the innocent friction between our bodies. I finally made it through the crowd and had to do a double-take to make sure what I was seeing was real. Adam was sitting on another guy's lap. Not only was he sitting on another guy's lap, but the guy's hand was placed firmly on Adam's hip. This took me as a surprise not so much that Adam was gay, but more so that I didn't connect the dots sooner. I contemplated just leaving The Crowd as not to embarrass him or put him on the spot. It was too late. Our eyes were locked. It was intense and uneasy. I thought about acting like I had suspected all along, and this was no surprise to me. It was futile, as always I wear my emotions on my sleeve.

Adam seemed fazed and got up and approached me. He grabbed me by the arm and pulled me into the men's restroom and into a stall. We stood there in close proximity to one another with our backs up against the walls. Adam stood there with his hand on his chin as he searched for the words.

"I want to be normal." These words finally forced their way out of Adam's fixed lips. He rubbed his forearm vigorously and when he wasn't doing that he began to bite his fingernails to the point where he must have been tasting flesh.

"You are normal. Don't be dumb, it's not like I am really all that surprised."

"Bullshit! I saw the look on your face when you saw me. All those weekends at my cottage when the four of you would swap sex stories. I just sat there and thought about if I would ever be able to open up to you guys," Adam said as his eyes welled up and his voice cracked.

"Adam, you're normal. We are normal." This was the only truth I could convey, which might be of comfort to him.

"Fuck, Jack. If you're normal, then count me out. You are anything but normal. I have practiced this speech so many times. I knew one day I would either get caught or come out."

"Ya it felt a bit rehearsed." I replied to him.

We both laughed, and I realized that my comment wasn't based on truth, but on empty comfort. He was right. In this stall stood two complete social weirdoes, one for his sexual orientation and another because he chose to be odd. We spoke for a bit longer without really saying anything of worth but I could see Adam's comfort level rise like a powerful tide. It was unnecessary to discuss his personal life, for he didn't need to explain anything to me. I swung the stall door open and we exited, Adam wiped away his tears between fits of laughter. He knew even if I was straight, he had an ally to stand with him along the sidelines of accepted society.

"Feel free to tell the other guys," said Adam as he lifted his head, in what I could only assume was a restoration of pride, the first time I could ever sense true pride in him.

Chapter 14

The news of Adam's secret made me feel less alone in the world. Less ostracized, as if his choice allowed me to push off the wall of the outskirt and enter the ring of society. I can't believe this made me happy; I had loved my place on the sidelines. I brought my own lawn chair and had the best seat in the house to watch the war of the elite. If being normal was my desire, then why did I end it with Catherine?

My day had soured, and I went to the only place where I was sure there would be someone to talk to. I sat in my usual place, and he sat in his. I had the same tone and mannerism as always, as did he. We had grown an evident comfort for each other, and there was no need for pleasantries or to be phony.

"So your friend is gay. Is that what is bothering you, Jack?"

"You know very well that it's not," I replied, and he knew that I had no problem with homosexuality. No matter how liberal of a priest he is, I will always have him beat in that department.

"You are not happy when you are different. You're not happy as soon as you begin to feel normal. I don't know if I'll ever understand you, Jack. You're an anomaly, a miscalculation in the system. Someone forgot to carry the zero," the priest said to me. I think he understood me though, he probably knew me from the core of my soul to the very end of my fingertips. He had a propensity not to give me the encouragement I sought. I felt as if he made a conscious effort to do this. He was elusive, and I don't know if he just wanted me to figure myself out, or if in actuality, I was a mystery to him.

"How's Megan?"

"No idea."

"And Catherine--"

I tried my hardest to remain calm at his line of questioning. I was feeling calmer than I had in passed visits.

"They're all shit. They're all great. I honestly have no idea," I said. The priest was a little taken aback by my calmness. He had come to expect some sort of outburst. The priest paced back and forth, knowing full well that patience was not only a virtue but a job requirement. He searched for the something to say, as he saw that beneath my tranquility, something was off. He gazed at me as if in that one conversation I had gone from being a reclamation project to a lost cause. After months of conversing, we had reached a point, a point where he might have realized that I cannot be reached. I didn't want to believe this. I came to him because I wanted to change, and he was cheaper than a shrink. Over the duration of our months of meeting together, I felt we were similar enough in nature, that he would understand me, even if I didn't understand myself most of the time.

This Church had become my own personal sanctuary. It was my castle or kingdom, if you will, and within its walls I had dominion over all creatures. The Church was always empty, and, over time, I began to realize that the emptiness was why the priest chose this venue. He could be a priest without ever having to exercise the role of a priest. It was his get out of jail and into heaven free card. Jail and heaven are two words that constantly bump into one another. To get into heaven your physical life has to be a prison of averted temptation and constant adoration. There is little room for actual living. Is heaven such a great party that it is worth it to make life so bland?

The priest finally broke the silence. "Life isn't as bad as you make it, Jack."

"Look around, priest. Look at this concrete paradise you label as 'not so bad'. I see nothing when I stare out my window; absolutely nothing. I see people beyond repentance, a landscape demolished and overdeveloped, and I see a world so devoid of culture and connectivity that we applaud the slightest innovation as human progress," I said to the priest, in my calmest voice that I summoned from within me. I lowered my head and stared at the ground awaiting his response. My eyes had welled up and I didn't want him to see. My usual anger had become replaced with sadness.

"Jack, as you name all the shit you see, you could find positives in the world even on this campus. Even in times of war and depression, people find a way to manage. It is almost as if you wished that your generation had something of that effect. It would justify their actions for you."

"Where did you get that gem?" I said to the priest. I found his statement a bit odd, but I recognized the inherent truth of what he was saying.

"Well, Jack, I should get going and have some dinner. Would you like to join me?" The priest extended his invitation. I was drained though and kindly had to reject his offer.

We went our separate ways without uttering goodbyes. The priest went behind the altar and retreated to the tiny apartment given to him by the Church. He didn't even turn back to see if I made my way out. He simply knew that I came and went as I pleased. The sanctity of the Church hung over and trailed after me like smoke, even after I had passed through the doorway. It's only a building, yet it made me feel grossly inferior. I walked down the hall, which felt as if it was growing increasingly narrow. Colors swirled and penetrated my retinas causing me to cringe from the offensive brightness. The stress was getting to me; the stress from this so-called holy place and from my life was weighing my senses down. I had to sit down somewhere.

The day started with promise. I broke out of one prison to enter right back into my prior one. There was no escape and no pardon or reprieve on its way. Love didn't bring me happiness nor did the plight of others. I felt trapped, and the priest even lost the magic of his company. Every time we met became shorter, and his patience had begun to dissipate. My life had become decorated with a self-imposed bar motif, and all I could do was sit on a bench and attempt to collect myself.

The wind picked up and grabbed hold of my hair. The breeze was nature's comfort to me right now. I leaned back and looked out onto the vibrant campus. This campus was a microcosm of society, and, as always, I was on the periphery. Did I want to be? And if so why was I so upset then? I was witnessing the actions of so many people, but I felt as if they were worth more than I made them out to be. I stared at the ivy-laced bricks of the chemistry building in front of me. The unified, red, crumbling bricks made up the oldest building on campus. It was dilapidated and completely unaesthetic, and to make matters worse it was surrounded by newer, brighter, innovative and postmodern buildings. Eventually it would make way for a new chemistry building, and the administration would hail it as progress and a sign of prosperity for the college.

My body was beginning to relax, and my mind was following its inspiration, so I figured I dared not move from this bench. I had a mental montage of my conversations with the priest, and all the different things he had said or revealed to me. He was a very bare individual, a minimalist both emotionally and in worldly possessions. He had lost everything that he held dear, things my generation takes for granted. For something to have value for us, it has to have resale value on eBay. The priest would never have fit into my cohort. I suppose he would have been who I am now. My admiration for him became dread as I saw his life as a crystal ball into my future. When I could not take anymore, would I turn to the Church for salvation? That would be a complete 180 degree turn for me. I could not fathom this idea; it would never happen as I found no solace in what that particular institution offers. I went to the Church because of the priest, not because of the faith. I'd set up shop in the desert before I ever got ordained.

After my period of lethargic empathy on the bench, I headed back to my dorm room for a much needed rest. An exhausting day as so many of my days at college had been. Uneventful and filled with questions, doubt and anxiety to the point I felt as exasperated as most athletes do after a big game. I needed sober rest.

Chapter 15

It was dark yet comforting. There was not an eerie ambience to it at all. Unlike most dreams, I had awareness of my actions and of the fact that it was a departure from reality. I stood clothed in a meadow with a warm wind rushing past my still body. The meadow was completely adrift in an endless ocean. I was surrounded by grassy hills, far removed from any human traffic and basking in the bright glow of the sun. In the distance, I could sense some sort of civilization and its attributes. I could faintly hear the bustling of urban life, the coldness and the emotional vacuum that accompanied its day-to-day activities. I was delved deep into solitude, unable to even enter back into the societal fray. I was alone, unassimilated and an island unto myself. Only my senses would ever wash ashore, not a soul would visit or stumble upon this meadow.

It was probably only a fraction of a second long, yet it dragged on for what seemed like hours. It was lush in detail and rich in its texture. As I stared out of the isolated meadow, I could see the world drifting away, as if its anchor had rusted through and snapped. The further the world floated away from my grasp, the louder I could hear the voices emanating from inside it. They were not calling for me, only bellowing as if entrapped in a floating prison. The voices grew and bounced off the water and smacked my brain. The waves carried them towards me at a constant and frustrating rate.

I could make out a few of the distraught voices; there were the voices of the priest, Catherine, Megan, my father, and others who had drifted in and out of my life. I sat on the shores of my island and waited for something to happen, even though I knew nothing ever would. I waited and waited, and I pondered and pondered. I prayed to whomever that the voices of those I knew would linger, but, as time went on, they continued to dissipate into the eternally vast landscape. The voices were lost in air currents and through water vapor in the sky, and, as it began to rain, the droplets would splash on the flowers in my meadow, and I could hear their voices cry in agony. Megan's voice rang the loudest, and it permeated my brain and my nerves. Who was a prisoner? I, Jack, was alone and removed. They were trapped in a world I wanted no part of, but they had each other and a chance at redemption. The sun rises, the sun sets, and each day can bring forth the promise of change. I, alone in a meadow, would have no such agency or no need for it.

To my own sadness, the voices had faded from the meadow. I could no longer hear Megan, Catherine, the priest, my father, or any of the other distinct or anonymous voices. I ran as fast as I could to the edge of the meadow and stopped on a dime. The warm breeze remained, and I could hear its whistling grow louder and louder. I sat down on the cool ground and immediately noticed that the blades of grass had lifted up all the way to my neck. The breeze forced each blade to brush up along my body and to create a symphony of senses.

I stared out towards the vast body of water and hoped that what appeared like civilization would return. I just wanted to see it, that's all. I could not decide if I was happier on this meadow, but I did know that some part of me missed hearing the voices. I watched the waves move back and forth from civilization to where I was and I hoped that they would bring a familiar sounding syllable to my meadow. Despair began to grow within me, and I had no way to fight the rising feeling. The sun continued to shine brightly on the small piece of unpopulated land, and I coupled that with the breeze to try and calm myself down.

I finally awoke around noon. I had complete recollection of the dream, even though some of the detail had already exited my subconscious. For a dream, it was quite detailed and memorable. I cannot remember the last time that I could recall any part of any dream so vividly. I remained in bed, thinking, trying so hard to piece what I remember together and even attempted to jot it down. I knew it was startling on some level. I closed my eyelids so tightly in order to remember every sight and sound. I even tried falling back asleep in order to pick up where I left off. Trying to remember any further detail of the dream was pointless, so I got out of my bed.

I became preoccupied with other things. My mother and stepfather were coming up to visit me for the afternoon. I had been dreading this day since September, but there was no talking her out of it. I was to meet them at a restaurant on the periphery of the east end of campus at around 1 o'clock for lunch.

I was all set to go and headed out of Drake, towards the restaurant. I walked past the Tubor memorial, and I could tell how it was dwindling into obscurity. Flowers were dying, and the notes had been blown or kicked away. Interest in it had evaporated, and no one even spoke of that day or mentioned the name Randy Tubor. Heartbreak became fascination, which became faint interest, which became a memory, which had now dried up. I didn't even stop to embrace this thought, which I knew I could revel in, because it is why I hate the inhabitants of this college. I kept walking with absolutely no interest in dissecting the aftermath of the Tubor incident.

I arrived at the restaurant, and I bent down to tie my shoe. As I did this, I noticed my stepfather's car parked outside the restaurant. It was a silver Acura that would forever be etched in my memory. I'll never forget the night that I endeavored to steal it, only to be caught as I was opening the garage door. My stepfather was a slim man and dainty in his features. In fact, he was not very masculine at all. He was a pencil pusher for an insurance agency, and my mother was already his third wife before he had entered his mid-forties. He was once widowed and once divorced and had no children to show from either marriage. I believe as deep down to my core as far as my conviction would travel that he wanted the financial security of marrying my widowed mother. There was simply no doubt in my mind. He is an asshole and a complete parasite. That night in the garage, he struck me across my face. My mother was soundly asleep, and he and I were alone and left to his devices. He cursed and berated me and only then, through the outlet of his anger, he would confide in me how he despised me and my mother and everything about our "insipid" lives. He even cursed out my dog. From that moment, I knew my time at home was going to come to an end shortly, and I looked forward to it. I told my mom of the events that had transpired that night, and the only part of the story she believed was the part where I tried to steal the car.

After that night, living at home was similar to renting a room in some posh hotel. I left without uttering a word and returned at will and was never questioned about where I was going or where I had been. It progressed to the point where my house became the place where everyone wanted to hangout, due to the lack of parental supervision. We would smoke and snort drugs in my room and would never worry about someone barging in or even knocking on my door. My friends and I would sometimes spend days in my room without even thinking of leaving.

I stood back up and walked towards the front door of the restaurant. I could already see them sitting in a booth, looking as cold and distant from one another as I felt to them.

"Hey, Jacky."

"Hi Mom. How are you? Hey, Jon," I said trying to be as indifferent to him as possible. "How was the drive?"

"It was fine Jack, have a seat and let's order already," my mom said as we sat down and they both reached for a menu.

"You don't look so good, bud. You're sniffing a lot," Jon said as he peered into my eyes, trying to coax some sort of confession out of me. He had been a cokehead as well back in the day, so he knew I didn't have a cold.

"What does that mean? Jack, are you sick or something? Jon, stop staring at him like that, he's not on trial." My mom stepped in, even though she was oblivious to what our exchange meant.

"I'm fine, Mom. Let's just order."

The waiter arrived and took our orders. I was not overly hungry, but I knew if I didn't order a normal size meal that it would arouse his suspicion. The food arrived, and we all dug in. My mom kept asking questions about school, and I kept feeding her bullshit about how I was excelling, when in truth I hadn't stepped inside a lecture hall in days if not weeks. I just didn't care.

"Are you seeing any girls right now?" Jon asked me. Guess he was looking for a reason to give me a high five or something generic like that.

"Sort of, we just broke up a few days ago. See how it goes, I suppose."

"What's her name?" My mom asked hoping that she was nice and could be good for me.

"Catherine, but like I said we'll see how it goes."

"Okay, I hope it works out. Have you met a lot of people this year?"

"Ya I've made some friends here and there, one in particular."

"That's great. You can't spend all your time with Peter, Luke, and Mark." My mother said to me and eagerly awaited my answer.

"Well, actually, he's the priest at the campus church." I refused to raise my head from my food to see their expressions.

"Don't priests usually hang out with younger boys than you, Jack?" The asshole said to me.

I heard the snap, and I smashed my plate on the brown plastic table just hard enough that it made a fierce sound but didn't break. Then it fell to the floor and shattered into a dozen pieces upon impact. I leaned over from my seat and lunged at Jon. I grabbed him by his starched collar and his shirt became interwoven into my fingers. I shook mercilessly as my anger towards his ignorance infuriated me. To hell with his ignorance, that priest was twice the man he was, and no less would be the second of the two to ever harm a child. I had to attack him and I had to do it before he could let out one of his arrogant and snaky laughs. I wouldn't stand for it.

"Jack! Get off of your father now," my mother bellowed as the restaurant looked on in confusion as to what the ruckus was all about. My mother began crying and knew this was a mistake. I was older now and would not shy away from his comments and actions.

"Fuck you, Jack. I should cut you off," Jon said.

"It's not even your money, Jon. It's my father's money, you corporate asshole." I yelled to him as my voice became raspy and dry. He knew exactly what I was referring to as well.

"How many promotions have you gotten in twenty years? You insignificant fuck," I said as he stared at me, refusing to blink.

He was corporate wallpaper, his ambition great, but he was always passed over time and time again for any promotion. He was known around my household for his transference of anger. He was constantly disappointed with his professional life and constantly took it out on my mother and me.

"Let's leave," he said as I released him from my grip. I stood there breathing heavily.

"Jon, I want to see my son."

"I'm leaving. Your son can go to hell."

Jon left the restaurant and sat in the car. He turned it on, and the exhaust matched the steam rising from the top of his head. My mother stood in front of me.

"Don't worry about money. I should have told you this a long time ago, Jack, but I know Jon was a mistake. I would leave him but I would lose the money, and I wouldn't be able to help you. You're father was a good man. I screwed up, Jack."

I had nothing to say back. She was preaching to the already converted. I loved her, and I could live with her mistake. I would tell her to just burn the money and leave, but it was futile. She walked away without a hug, a kiss, or even a goodbye. It was fitting to say the least. This was what our relationship had come to since I was fifteen years old, and I didn't know if there any moving forward or going back.

Chapter 16

That lunch stayed with me for the entire day. I hated him so passionately. I could never hate her, though. And then there is my father... I will never forget that morning I awoke to the sound of ambulances and fire trucks screeching into my driveway. I had no idea what was going on. He was getting dressed for work--then he was lying face down, and his olive colored skin was a light, cold shade of blue. The sirens constantly pierce me, and I can never stop hearing them in the background. It is a tumor lodged in my body festering and feeding on pure animosity. There is no cure for it.

I sat alone in my room contemplating the afternoon. Memories flooded my brain of growing up in that household. Those memories were replaced with thoughts of Megan and how she was these days. I had not seen her since the night we spent together, and I had figured she left school shortly after being raped. I began to wonder if maybe she was pregnant or something stupid like that. I hoped I would never see her again; there is no way I am eloquent or comforting enough to know what to say to her. It was best if we didn't cross paths again, at least for awhile. This endless stream of thoughts, memories and bullshit made me reach into my drawer and search for a CD case, a straw cut in half and the white powdery substance. I even had a quick look to see if there was any weed or shake lying in the drawer. The drawer was bare, and I don't know if I was relieved that I had no choice but to be sober or upset because I really wanted to get high.

I swirled in my chair and stared idly at my stucco ceiling. After a little while my door swung open, and, in one motion, Peter and Luke entered into my room. As Luke walked past me, he gave me a friendly slap on the shoulder, and they both proceeded to sit on my bed. The three of us sat there and spoke, and, even though it went against my common sense, I told them about what I had learned about our old friend Adam. Peter let out a nervous laugh, while Luke looked as if he was awaiting a nuclear bomb to detonate.

My two oldest friends and I moved our conversation into the common room, and we sat there for hours. We spoke nostalgically of our years in high school together and our first few months away at college. Peter confronted Luke about his addictions and then berated me for following in his misguided footsteps. I was in no mood to be looked down upon. I sat there on the floor cross-legged as Peter would recount stories of nights wasted as we got high and waxed poetically on nothing. He spoke of the worry and fear he felt of where our lives would go, and he even spoke of the worry he felt when I was hit by that cyclist months ago. Funny enough, I had almost forgotten about that incident.

I was tempted to tell them of my relationship with the priest. It was completely innocent, yet I know how our young and jaded minds work. The hour was reaching into the early morning, and I was losing focus on what Peter had been saying. Once I thought of the priest and things he would say to me, my mind drifted endlessly. He always compelled me by either revealing information about himself or by giving insight into myself of which I was previously unaware. I usually disregarded it at the time, but it had a prolonged lingering effect. I knew I was scared to be happy for whatever stupid reason I had conjured up in my mind, and I knew that eventually I would have to combat it. I would just keep trying to get myself to buy into the world I perceived around me, but it was hard for me to buy in when I never originally sold out.

I grabbed a piece of pita and dipped it into the humus we had set out on the coffee table. As I ate and listened to Luke and Peter, I realized that I had allowed my friendships with them to almost vanish as I spent my time doing coke, smoking weed and thinking. Peter kept directing questions my way in an attempt to figure out what had been happening to me the past few months. Between Catherine, drugs and the priest, I had barely uttered a word around our suite.

Peter's voice rattled through the halls, and eventually Mark woke and joined us in the common room. I stared at him until I could sense him notice me out of his peripheral vision, and I realized that in some way he looked different to me. He looked fresh in my eyes, and I began to pickup his nuances. The same nuances I had grown accustomed to and had been annoyed with so many times in high school. The hand gestures he used when he spoke or the way his nostrils flared when he laughed even the slightest. It was all coming back to me. Peter and Luke sat on the couch, and Mark and I sprawled out on the floor on the other side of the coffee table.

This was the first time the four of us had been together in the same room in weeks. Whenever this occurred, I could not help but remember back to the four years I had spent in a high school in suburban Seattle. There was the flood of anxiety on the first day, the fake sentimentality of the last day, and all the rites of passages in between. High school for me was about achieving predetermined clichés, whereas now I was dying to create distance between those flawed achievements and the new, college Jack Geary. I hated myself in high school, and it was a process for me to learn to deal with myself once I left it. My friends never seemed to question who they were. If they ever felt out of place, it was easy for them to simply repress any introverted ill will.

I would walk through the pale yellow hallways as a ghost and would observe the cliques and their self-quarantined hangouts. Goths, Ravers, Preppies, Jocks, Nerds, and Druggies lined the hallways and existed as oil and water would if they attended secondary school. The Goths never spoke to the Jocks, who never looked at the Nerds, who would only dream of dating the Preppies.

I remembered nights spent getting high and drunk in recreational parks where we would discuss the pointless absurdities and banalities of day-to-day life. It was excruciating, but ultimately it was fun. Peter,

Luke, Mark, Adam, and I would expunge the shallow cores of our adolescent depths amidst the backdrop of a twilight infested park for hours on end. We were as pretentious as any other clique; just lacked gimmicky appeal. In retrospect, if we had known then that Adam was gay, we could have played that angle up, but it would have only marginalized us even more. On the sidelines of popularity, we had each other, and it was more than enough to allow us make it through those four years. Unfortunately for us, it also meant we had to find a way to spend college together since our social skills never fully developed outside of our circle.

My memories came to a halt, and I entered back into the moment and the conversation at hand. Peter was still on the topic of my drug use and my behavior over the last few months. I was silently praying that the name Catherine would not enter into the conversation. I had not spoken to her since the night that I ended our relationship. I don't know if it was pride that was keeping me from contacting her. All I knew was that I missed her so much. She was that entity that the priest spoke of which allowed people to sustain themselves through wars and economic hardship. I was a fool to have given her up.

Peter continued to facilitate discussion as the hours passed and I sat there lost in my own thoughts. I usually got so caught up in the past that the future seemed irrelevant. I began to wish that thoughts of the future would begin to drown my brain, and the past could be placed where it was always intended to be.

As Peter continued to speak to a captive audience of three, I immediately realized that this was his role amongst our group. He was extremely prone to lecturing us whenever one of us stepped out of line. He gave up on Luke years ago, when he realized that Luke needed drugs to deal with who he was. I could see that he thought I was different than the average drug user. He thought I did it because I merely wanted to do drugs. He was there when I first tried cocaine, and it was the only time that he would ever try it himself. We had been at the after prom party for the students who were a few years older than we were. Luke and Mark had to work that night, so Peter and I headed down by ourselves to a party where we only knew each other.

We arrived at the motel and immediately became wallpaper for the cooler kids to lean up against as they drank and hit on anyone in their vicinity. Finally, out of the noise and debauchery, an arm was extended to us. The hand of that arm unfolded, and resting comfortably on the palm was a gorgeous powder. The arm belonged to a student named Gordon Brody, and he was always willing to get the younger students immersed in a new lifestyle, even if the new lifestyle was deadly. Gordon brought Peter and me over to a coffee table in the center of the room and on it he placed five small bumps for us to devour. We sat down, and I gave Peter a look to see if he was actually going to do it, and he didn't even bother looking back as he plunged his face into the line of coke.

I watched in awe as Peter hit three of the five slender lines. After a few brief seconds, he jerked his head back as if attached to a taut tether rope and leaned back onto the couch. I followed suit and threw myself face first into the narcotic and without a single hesitation, I sniffed the two lines straight up my virgin nose. My nose became red, and a burning sensation crept up its passage into my mint brain.

Peter and I left the motel the next morning and didn't utter a word to each other on the way home. In retrospect, we should never have told Luke what we did that night. The way I romanticized the experience made his mouth water, and to this day it waters every time someone even mentions the word. Luke waited months before he approached Gordon in the hallways of our high school. Finally, he pulled him aside after class and asked him to hook him up, even if it was the weakest shit on the streets. Gordon complied and charged him one hundred and fifty dollars for a single gram. Translation for the non-cokehead: that is way more than it would cost an experienced user with half a brain.

Once Luke was hooked on coke, it gave me a reason to do it more frequently and that suited me just fine. Luke and I would bring vials of chopped rocks to classes and hit little lines whenever the teachers' eyes would be diverted. The smallest distraction always meant that we would have a small window of opportunity to place a bump on the area between our thumb and index finger, and inhale it as quickly as we possibly could without being noticed. We were successful each and every time.

This became common practice during the last two years in high school for Luke and me. Peter and Mark never dabbled in anything more than the odd joint, even though on many occasions I can recall the two of them getting drunk beyond their limits. Every student at that school seemed to be loaded most of time. Ecstasy, weed, coke, and hallucinogens flowed through the grimy halls of my public high school. Kids walked to class constantly gnawing their jaws and hoping not to swallow their pierced tongues. Glassy eyes were vacant, and clothes reeked of stale weed and the drinking binges of minors.

Since high school, my thoughts have been consistently muddled. As a child, I didn't have a single worry about the world or the people around me. I could focus on a blade of grass for hours and just listen to the wind whistling past it as it swayed in the breeze. As soon as I entered into the black hole of high school, every feeling, thought, and ounce of disenfranchisement became magnified. The music I listened to changed, the films I watched and books I read were different, and in the end I was a different person. I was a shadow of the scared and idealistic young man that I was when I first entered high school. This was all a natural process I suppose, but that doesn't mean that I had to embrace the new me.

I began listening to Pearl Jam and Nirvana shedding myself of the ease of listening to more radio friendly music. I was not interested in mainstream cinema as much, and I would allow the words of Dostoyevsky, Salinger and Capote to leap off the pages and induce some feeling within me to stir the numbness and force it to awaken. Organizing a game of street hockey with friends was replaced with getting high and hanging out with girls, which became more of a conquest than an innocent good time.

The conversation ended as sleep began to set in within the four of us. We got up and went to our separate rooms and went to sleep. I lay in my bed for a few minutes before my consciousness began to drift, and all I could think of was Catherine. My room was pitch black, and this was the first time in recent memory that I was going to sleep with the television off. I began to think about how alone we all are in this vast world but how at the same time we are connected. There are brief moments where you know that stranger on the subway or in the elevator is going through what you are, but they are different somehow and that difference becomes a barrier.

Chapter 17

For whatever reason, I decided to attend a lecture, and I arrived promptly in order to get a good seat. The lecture was for a course entitled "U.S. in the World," and centered on the foreign policy of this beloved, God-given country. The professor began his lecture to a half-empty auditorium. He was belligerent in his body language and poured information concerning the Monroe Doctrine and Brinkmanship. He spoke of the great leaders of this nation as they dragged us through war after war and campaign after campaign in order to prevent a domino effect or to rid the world of the communist cancer.

I couldn't help but think of all this history as complete bullshit. The history of the U.S. seemed an affront to good sense and humanity. A history laced with burning crosses, slavery, wars, Vietnam, the Middle East, intolerance blah, blah, blah. There were too many horrors to speak of. Suddenly, I heard something that has stuck with me to this very day.

"We act as if the momentum of history has brought us to this point in time. We act as if we have achieved as much as we can, technologically and scientifically, and this can not be so. Our species is merely a sliver in time, a blip on the radar screen and we must understand this. If the history of our species was a clock hanging on a wall, we would only be five past twelve."

"What the fuck!" I said this to myself, and his words rang in my ears and forced me to lean forward in anticipation. These words came out of nowhere, and the other times I had attended his lectures he was passionate but usually quite neutral. The professor's diatribe continued and he was adamant about his convictions, in a futile attempt to make my generation of educated elites humble. He spoke of Darwin, Huxley, and their detractors and his support of science over religion. His face became beet red as he outlined debates over evolution, eugenics, and phrenology. While he spoke, all I could picture was an analog clock hanging on a white wall. The hour hand was situated on the twelve, and the minute hand was trying to move past the five. What would happen when that minute hand would finally reach six or ten or forty?

The other students seemed unfazed by this proclamation. I couldn't decide if it was too complex or if this body of students had just tuned out a long time ago. I scanned the lecture hall and saw complete disinterest replace air as the students sketched on their notebooks, talked on their cells, or even watched movies on their laptops. Not an eyebrow rose amongst the two hundred or so students. I could sense the professor had taken notice of this, and what started out as passion for his vision had become the realization that he was lecturing to an intellectual black hole, where his voice exited his mouth and entered only in his own eardrum.

I was hooked though, and I would not let my apathetic peers lead me away from the catharsis of this moment. These words were unlike others which were spoken within this corporate campus. A lecture of verve, passion, and insight spoken from an unlikely source, a simple cog in the machine was completely unheard of. The machine of zombie-like, overpaid and detached faculty members that would do what they were told, and had abandoned the purity of academia long before I had entered into this world. This lecture was a rainbow visible in a puddle along a street. It was a reminder that we are not in a perpetually comatose state and that there are people who can be lucid.

Where did it come from? Out of the abyss of regurgitated garbage which inflicts the bored-shitless students came a string of words, a string which could not be broken or erased. He had articulated what I had been feeling for months, and yet I was unable to transform from a liquid into a solid. This felt like a resurgence of sorts.

I was saddened when the clock struck three and the lecture adjourned. I stared at the professor as he nonchalantly packed up his notes and turned the PowerPoint presentation off. He was remarkably intelligent and conveyed conviction in his beliefs. I sat in my seat and thought about what I had missed by not attending his lectures all year long. It made me want to kick my own ass for a brief second. It was as if he was a man possessed. The professor exited the hall, and I sat there staring at the flapping door, in fact I realized that I was the only soul left in the room.

We are just a blip on a radar screen. One day, our species will cease to exist and the next species will study us as we presently study the dinosaurs. I almost wished it was true.

Chapter 18

The next class began to filter into the lecture hall, and I decided it was time for me to leave. I had no intention of attending any other classes today and for a second I couldn't even remember if I had one. There was a buzz circulating the Student Center where I was hanging out, and I could hear people discussing something they were reading in the campus newspaper. I hustled over to the newsstand and grabbed the last edition before anyone else who was on the same course could. I flipped the top half of it up and brought it close to my eyes. All the enlightenment I had just endured abruptly left my body. A fear of mine had been realized.

My college was joining forces with a soft drink company and from here on out it would officially be corporately sponsored. To add insult to injury, they were renaming the old chemistry building after a land development firm. The Chemistry Building would be forever known as The Tetron Development Building. I was enraged and could feel my blood boil to a head. The veil of academia was now lifted, and a deadened and dark corporate factory had risen from the ashes of a once proud school. Students would be molded to become future CEOs and corporate appendages and superfluous corporate entities. History and the arts would be shoved so far past the backburner they wouldn't feel any heat.

I stood there as a calm center in a blur of activity. Students and support staff passed by me and carried on through their daily routines, and yet I stood there. Four years from now, I would not even give two shits about this place and I would be in the workforce somewhere. I would remember back harshly to my confused years spent as a college student and how, for once in my life, I actually gave a shit. Maybe I would even get a job in some nameless, faceless corporation somewhere in the U.S. Maybe I would adore that life. Maybe I would put a bullet in my temple from being so fucking happy all the time.

The Tetron Development Building had no ring to it--as if that mattered to the administrative committee who sold it. The money had exchanged hands and lined pockets, and that is what was vital. Fifteen million dollars was the price for a new building and naming rights, and Tetron was more than happy to fork it over. We would learn and expand our minds in any discipline we choose, under the ceiling and guise of a corporate sponsored education.

I remained in the Student Center and stared at the unfurled newspaper. The print appeared in bold letters to my trained eyes. The stench of the campus hung above me. It was growing in its potency and was becoming tangible. I finally lifted my head and saw, to my childish delight, that I was not alone in my disgust. Rows of students stood in the student center with a look on their face as if the Earth had been thrown off its axis. Eyes fixated on the same article that I was reading, and I could see dozens of students not shying away from emotion. Some students turned to each other and began discussing the ramifications of the Tetron sponsorship. The Student Center blistered with young malcontents, who were beginning to appear differently to me; and I could sense an atmospheric shift occurring.

Maybe we could finally unite against something. For once I could scan an area of campus and feel some sort of connection. It was a connection of dissatisfaction, but it was something, and it was the first time I had experienced this since I arrived at the college. It was only a few dozen students, but it was real. I felt giddy at this notion and the event which was transpiring. Maybe this time disinterest wouldn't replace dissatisfaction. The students were visibly upset. It wasn't just I, who thought that the actions of the administration were corrupt. I felt like I belonged with these people and that we could accept each other. I realized that all of this would take time, but I gladly accepted this exciting new development.

Wasted air circulated the surrounding area and infiltrated my nasal passages. It carried the scent of fast food, caffeine, and overpriced hair products. Metrosexuals, "Emo" kids and other newly unearthed stereotypes had blown into the Student Center from other parts of campus, and with them they brought in their afflictions and attempted to belong in this Mecca of commerce and education. It was an intersection you might approach on a street visited during those twelve thousand years spent in purgatory. The two words kept invading the electrical currents in my brain: education and commerce, commerce and education. From this day forth, they were lovers, and it would be a symbiotic marriage. I could only dare imagine what their children might look like.

I left the Student Center with a mixture of feelings, and I tried to resist any interest I had in sifting through them. I could not help but think that for a brief second there was a spark present. It faded though and the administration would ultimately do as they wished. It's only rape if you try to stop it, otherwise if you ask me you're just getting fucked. As I walked out, I could still hear voices stirring about the Tetron Development Building. I lit a cigarette and leaned myself up against a hurting tree whose branches had been spliced in order to not interfere with the passing of human traffic. I turned my attention to the other side of the Student Center and realized the differences in the two ends of the building. At one end was everything I hated about this insufferable campus and on the opposite end was where I would scurry to when it had become overwhelming. The end of the building had stained glass windows, which, if one was to look through, could see the one untouched area of the campus. Few ever took the pilgrimage to it, and even fewer ever fathomed the notion.

I saw no light beaming from the end of the building where the church was located. I heard no noise making its way out of the window. There was no aura or presence to it. The Church merely slid into the building and laid there dormant and lifeless. I continued smoking my cigarette and stood there trying to alter my field of vision. There was not much else to look at: a hot dog vendor, busses pulling in and students walking off them, and the push of water out of a fountain in the middle of main campus. The Church, unlike the campus, had a lingering beauty, which created a noticeable dichotomy with its environment. Many areas of the large campus were constantly changing, yet the church always remained untouched. I looked down to see that my cigarette was burning very slowly, too slowly for my liking. I didn't want to discard it. Being without it would only make me feel like lighting a new one. What a simple and stupid machine I was.

I switched my position on the trunk of the tree so that I could stare at something else, while I labored my way through smoking this butt. Now I faced away from the Student Center, and I found it much more pleasing to both my retinas and my olfactory senses. My back was to the building which housed both the Church and the Student Center, and I found this to be much more fitting, but there was one thing in my view which made me feel unsettled. I saw the remains of the Tubor memorial, and it made me feel nothing. I scanned the tops of buildings and saw how they were constructed. I remembered reading that they were built a certain way, so, if a protest ever broke out, they would be easy to connect in order to lockdown the campus and allow tanks and military officials to enter. This didn't affect me one bit either. It was what one of the rooftops reminded me of, I suppose. It was the catwalk which connected the main area of campus to the path near Drake, and I would take it often on my way home. Just below the catwalk was the computer building and the old chemistry building. That catwalk was where I bumped into Catherine for the first time. I could not see the exact area where her beautiful head met with my shoulder, but I knew it was there. It existed just as she and I existed once, and no construction or "progress" could ever erase what had once happened.

I was always apprehensive of venturing into places that would bring a flood of memories. I continued that trend as I looked away, towards the roof of some nondescript building. What was the point? I kept repeating to myself. I could not come up with an answer, so I figured I was just better off. The memory of her is still there. I wanted to know how Catherine was doing these days. She hadn't called me or contacted me in so long. I wondered if she was over me or just waiting for me to stop being an idiot. I sincerely hoped she wasn't over me. It reeked of my relationship with Jordyn prior to college, but it had felt different with Catherine.

Chapter 19

The students marched as if traveling through an invisible burning tunnel. They were battle scarred, weary, and ultimately drained. Girl followed boy who trailed a succession of other boys and girls. It was monotonous and never-ending, yet no one would succumb to the tiresome routine. From dorm room to coffee shop to class and so on and so forth. There was no stopping for a breath, only brief pauses to merely make the odd sexual advance or check a cell phone or palm pilot. Young and programmed to an eerie beat. Their contempt was indistinguishable, and their happiness seemed like an untreatable illness. If one is happy but pretends to be angry because it is chic, are they as vacuous as an inherently angry person who consistently acts happy? Bullshit either way, I suppose.

I could watch them all day. I could observe their eyes being activated by the flash of billboards and digital signs. Moving in their monosyllabic manner; soulless and arrogant. The arrogance I assume was towards their parents' fiscal accomplishments and their already golden futures. I, for the most part, had similar assurance. That is, if Jon doesn't piss it away. No assurances then, I guess, but a worst (best) case scenario could see me becoming a farmer somewhere in Southern France for little pay. That would be something. To have the opportunity to stare out at a field and see no exhaust, would be worth the risk of being in a shitty tax bracket. I don't know where these thoughts came from, but they constantly plagued me. I gave my head a shake and tried to remain grounded in reality. Thoughts like that were simply useless to me right now.

I found them to be annoying; they had pedigree but lacked such vital cognitive functioning. When did we lose it? That pulse, that verve. The tenacity to be different is dried up. When exactly did the fear set in? The desensitization not only to the horrors of the world, but to anything the world has to offer. Good and bad have no effect on us. A plane flies into a building or a dog saves a little boy's life we just turn the television off and continue eating our preserved dinners. What does it take to make my generation care? These thoughts continued to blossom in my frail and stupid little head. Every other day was spring in my brain.

I leaned up against my tree in my usual pose and sawed a cigarette in and out from between my pursed lips. I wondered if I had developed OCD over the course of the last year. I had begun to do with things without reason with machine-like movements. The sake of doing certain things replaced purpose. Smoking was no longer done out of enjoyment nor was hating the fellow students on this campus. It was all the poetry of my daily routine. Some mornings I barely recognized myself. I used to smoke and do drugs because it was fun, but it lost most of its luster. I told the priest of the emerging trend in my habits. He was less than pleased but not the least bit surprised.

He would look at me with the stare of a discerning father. The same look my mother gave me while I was growing up and the same look Catherine gave me when I fucked up. I knew it all too well. It had practically become sunlight to me. I hadn't seen the priest in a while, and I reasoned with myself that a visit was definitely in order. I wondered what it would take to make our relationship strain as so many other relationships of mine have in the past.

I had officially grown tired of the watching the human assembly line, so I proceeded to the church. My usual path felt as mundane as any usual path should. I touched the walls as I stepped on each individual square on the parquet floor. The touch of the wall was appealing. It had a vibrant texture, and I had grown to appreciate such things.

I arrived at the gaping doors and, for the first time ever, the priest was already seated in a pew. He placed himself where I usually sat and waited. I stood at the doorway and wondered what my next move should be. Every time I had entered his workplace, he was in his apartment and eventually would make his way out once he was alerted that I had arrived. He sat there fully robed and sunken in the pew as if it was devouring him. From the back, he appeared dejected and in an odd and ambiguous way. Was he resting? Or was he upset? It was time I approached him and found out what the deal was. I walked slowly, then realized surprising him was a stupid idea, one which made me give off a little laugh. He noticed me as soon as I took a more solid step towards his pew.

"Jack."

"Hey." I took a seat next to him. The pew was awkward to sit on, but I knew that was its intended purpose, so I tried my best to pay no attention to it. This conversation desperately needed an ice breaker, and I felt bringing up the comfort of the pews was a solid one.

"You should do something about these seats."

"It's on my list," the priest replied.

"So what's wrong? I mean I walk in here, and it looks as if you're praying or something."

"Jack, you realize I am a priest and praying is part of my vocation. Would you be surprised if you walked into an auto shop and saw a mechanic with his head under the hood of a car?"

"No, of course not. Sorry, I know you're a priest. I have just never seen you so solemn in prayer before." I was embarrassed by my original surprise. There was no reason that I should have been taken aback by the sight of the priest in quiet prayer. I always assumed he was like me and, in doing so, I forgot that first and foremost he is a man of God. He was always more than a simple servant in my eyes and this was problematic. To me, he was mere flesh and blood.

"So what brings you here Jack?"

"What always brings me here, priest? I have no idea. The Lord works in mysterious ways or some shit like that."

"He always seems transparent to me. They are just old wives' tales, Jack." I noticed a complete change in his demeanor. He was different today then he was during previous encounters throughout the year. I wished I could put my finger on it. He was not an upbeat man, but he was usually collected and tranquil.

"I am thinking about leaving the campus for a bit, Jack. Maybe I won't do this line of work for a few months or so. Give something else a shot."

"C'mon, priest. That's bullshit. Where are you going to go? I mean this line of work isn't something you can just walk away from. Is it because of your wife?" I was hesitant to ask but I could not think of any other catalyst for this decision.

"Not really. I mean, ultimately, I am sure it traces to her, but it's this campus and these students. They don't get it, they don't get anything. You were right."

"I guess." My words became less frequent as his began to fill the church.

"They don't give a shit about this place or me. It's worthless to even try. I entered into the priesthood to hide from the world, but I thought I would at least have the chance to communicate to someone, to feel something. It has failed. I'm a dinosaur, Jack."

"They'll convince some other pointless priest to come here, and he'll think that he can change a bunch of students' lives, and it'll become cyclical. You know how it'll go." The priest spoke while only moving his thin lips. I saw it in him, the lack of emotional restraint. He was about to let it go after months of just handing out advice and listening to me yammering on. From time to time, he showed me glimpses into his past. I pieced most of it together rather haphazardly with makeshift precision, but I knew what he was about.

I was at a complete loss for words. I should never be the one to console another person during a time of trouble. As I searched for the right words, I could see rain streaming down the stained glass windows of the church. The rain fell down relentlessly and created a loud crashing sound as it collided with the window. The weather outside illuminated the image in the stain glass window, an image of a flock of sheep being led over a grassy hill by a shepherd. My eyes left the window and returned to the priest. He had not said a word in a few minutes now. His eyes were sunken into his skull, and his hands firmly gripped the material covering his knees. His breathing sped up, and I could see him make a conscious effort to slow it down.

The room grew humid as the weather outside made the temperature inside the church rise. I grabbed at my collar and pulled it forward until it was taut, in an attempt to release some of the heat accumulating underneath my shirt.

"Are you going to be here next fall, Jack?" said the priest without lifting his head to look at me.

"It's not my preference, but I don't see what other choice I have."

"You have options. You are young. You can do whatever you want."

This comment by the priest made me feel elated. I realized that the priest refused to make eye contact with me because it reminded him of opportunities lost. There was a point in his life where he had options and choices, but those days were gone. He should be enjoying his last years of molding young minds with his wife, but that life was taken from him. That night when I slept over at the priest's apartment after I broke up with Catherine, it was the first and only time he made mention of that day. When he recounted the story to me, I could sense the dread. It was the first time I genuinely felt sorry for another person. I mean, I know I have felt empathy for others but not to that degree and not in a long time. It made me sick to the pit of my stomach, hearing his story made me feel as if I was growing while the apartment rapidly shrunk. It was an utterly nauseating experience.

Say something please, I kept repeating in my head over and over again.

"You could join the military."

"Are you insane? I wouldn't last a single day." I had trouble believing the absurdity of his suggestion.

"The military. Sorry, Jack. I don't know what I was thinking. Just a generic piece of advice I would give to anyone. I forgot who I was talking to."

He paused for a quick second to gather his thoughts. He inhaled and exhaled a few times. "Why is it that the people who see things clearly are the ones who are miserable? Why are the uninformed so happy in such trite delights? I search this campus so deeply, and I see no mention of anything important. I don't see anyone who is concerned with anything other than technology or getting some remedial job when they graduate. They don't see the bleakness that exists even on the sunniest day. I wonder why the country just doesn't implement a one party system. Why give any of these people a chance to make a difference in the world? No one ever steps foot in this sanctuary because they don't realize they need heavenly guidance. They don't realize this life might be meaningless. Maybe it isn't meaningless. Maybe this world is the world we should be living for, but, if it's not, there will be an entire generation lost to an eternity in hell."

"Do you believe all of this?" I replied to him as I tried to make sense of his fractured thoughts. I knew what his point was and that I agreed with it, but he was on a different plane of thinking now, one that I could not tap into.

"I don't know, Jack. I suppose sometimes I genuinely do," the priest said before another long pause.

"Peace and order, order and peace. That's what makes the world go round. If someone breaks the harmony, they are a menace to society. These menaces can be writers, painters, sculptors, teachers, or anyone who ever looked around and didn't see some man-made utopia. Why do we have to fall in line? Can't we see the world for what it is, without being a cynic?"

He stopped speaking for about a minute and stared blankly towards the front of the Church.

"We had paradise Jack, a complete and untouched paradise, and we threw it all away. We threw it all away for nothing. For concrete, skyscrapers, cement, condos, country clubs, freeways and high rises. Paradise lost. How stupid we are, people wanting to colonize on Mars instead of fixing what we have now. Imagine that, Jack. Colonizing a new planet and eventually squeezing it dry and then eventually running out of planets. We'll have to find wormholes to new universes to find new planets until there is nothing left. No world, no planets, no universe, and no home."

"Does this shit keep you up at night? We have been going down this route for a very long time. There is too much momentum to divert the course," I said to him as realism hauntingly filled the church.

"This campus and these people just kill me." I said to him as I lit another cigarette. The priest didn't even flinch as the smoke floated in between us.

"You'll learn soon enough that people are empires unto themselves, Jack. We rise, we sustain as best we can through good times and hardships and eventually we all fall."

We sat there only a few feet apart, but our minds had finally fallen into sync. Even though we were feeling the same way, I was content with allowing the feeling to simply take over and drown me. The priest looked despondent and withdrawn. I am sure he must have had these realizations in the '70's, but now he was drained of any agency he once had. Sara must have taken it with her to the grave.

"So what the hell are you going to do now?"

"Collect some government cheques. Maybe I'll even write a little. If not, I'll just read a lot. I haven't touched a lot of great writers in a long time. I'll figure it out. I'm an old man, so maybe the world won't expect much from me anymore," said the priest as he straightened out his back and finally looked at me. He appeared less upset than when I first entered his place of work. He stared at my face for a few stretched out moments; moments that I hoped wouldn't end because I realized our time together was going to end very soon. I could not picture what my second year at college would have been like without him or if another priest was stationed here. This man who bestowed the campus with his grace was not an idealistic man nor was he a fundamentalist; he was just a man in priest's clothing. A sheep in wolf's clothing. However you cut it, he was my friend.

"You'll learn to accept this place, Jack, and one day your kids will go through the same thing when they are in college. It is completely natural."

"I don't know if I can ever get used to this place. Eventually something has to give. Four years in this place isn't going to work for me. I can just drop out."

"You'll be homeless."

"I'll be happy."

"It's not how things work."

"Fuck it."

The priest was torn between giving me the advice he felt he had to, and what he really believed was right. If I dropped out of college, my future was going to be limited, but, if I stayed in school, I would become one of them. A double edged sword dangled between me and both paths that I could have travelled.

"Do you still dream of the floating meadow, Jack?"

"All the time, priest."

He paused for a long moment and I could see his bottom lip trembling. I had nothing more to say to him, so I stood up and began to slowly walk away. While I was still in earshot I could perfectly hear the last words he ever uttered to me.

"Take care of yourself, Jack Geary."

Chapter 20

From the moment I woke up, I had convinced myself that today would be a bad day. Such a silly thing for anyone to do. I thought that without having the church to go to, I was stuck with just a campus. I left my room immediately to grab a coffee on campus. I walked right past Luke, Mark, and Peter who were hanging out in the common room watching television.

I felt relaxed as I sipped my coffee and flipped through the campus newspaper. As I sat there, I knew eventually I would run into someone I knew. Before I could finish my coffee, Adam appeared to me as he made his way to class.

He sat with me for a good solid hour and we spoke rather candidly. He told me about the guy whose lap he had been sitting on at The Hound, and about how they had been dating since October. Without hesitation, he told me about their sex life, which at first was odd to hear, but eventually it seemed as if he had been open about his sexuality since we were in grade nine. He looked exactly the same as he had back then, but his hair was even redder and his complexion smoother and more porcelain-like. I told him how I had told the other guys about his secret, and he seemed like a kid on Christmas morning. He appeared glad and relieved to know that the task was done.

Adam asked me about Catherine and tried to pry details out of me. The more he asked the more I realized that I wanted to be with her. I wanted to leap from my plastic seat and go find her. I don't know why I didn't, except that I was convinced that it was a matter of time before our paths would cross again. I missed her.

I told Adam about the priest and how he was gone now. Bless Adam for not asking me if I had some sort of sexual relationship. I rarely told people about us because I knew the conclusion people tend to jump to, and it infuriates me to no end. I told him about all of the talks the priest and I had, and I mentioned the floating meadow dream. Adam convinced me the symbolism was obvious, something I was already completely aware of. It was not a hard dream to decipher, but I really wished that it would stop haunting me whenever I closed my eyes. The voices in the raindrops became more pronounced with every dream.

Adam left for class. I got up and walked to the computer building to check my email. I hadn't checked it in a few days and figured, why not now? I had internet access in my dorm room, but I didn't feel like going home for awhile. I walked across campus, passed a dozen coffee shops and a hundred over-caffeinated students, and reached the computer building. I entered and saw thousands of computers lined up in little cubicles. I had to wait a little while for one to free up, but, once it did, I pounced on it. I sat down and logged in. To my surprise, I had an email that stood out from the normal spam and junk mail. It was from Megan. It read:

Dear Jack,

> *Sorry for leaving without saying bye. I won't be returning to school this year, and next year I will most likely be going to a state school in Ohio. I probably won't see you again, and I realize you probably won't respond to this email, but I felt that I had to contact you. I don't want to thank you, because I would hope anyone in your position would have done the same thing. I don't know, Jack. You should leave that school.*

Megan

As I read it, I could feel how cold of a person she had become since I last saw her. She was not the same person I had spoken to in that noisy hallway that day. I could not blame her, but I felt it was a shame. I began to wonder where the frat boy rapist was these days; I bet he hadn't changed one iota since that night. He had probably done it ten times since Megan.

Megan was right though. I didn't respond to the email then, nor did I have any intention to. I saw no good that could come from it. I contemplated for awhile whether or not I should just drop her a line, but it was pointless. I didn't know her anymore, and I was only a reminder of the moment when her life would never be the same again. Who needs that? She left before I had a chance to bring her to meet the priest. Now they were both gone for good.

I logged out of the computer and stood up. Immediately after I stood up, five students who had been swarming and eyeing me began to fight over who would get to use the computer next. It was quite the sight to see, very primal, a regression back to the good old days. It reminded me of a gold rush or a land drive that I had learned about in my history classes. Instead of getting hurt, I proceeded out of the computer lab and headed towards the outside of the building.

It was warm and bright out. In the distance I could see the walkway where Catherine and I had first bumped into each other. I watched as students walked back and forth across it. I don't think that they realized that if they walked fast and stared at the ground, they very well could fall in love. How often do the two same people bump into each other? Was that encounter my only chance with her? I figured at this point I would have to call or visit her if I wanted to reconcile, and that thought made me extremely nervous. Pride wasn't preventing me from admitting I was wrong. I felt that if I went back I would want to be with her forever. That was a scary endeavor.

In the opposite direction, I could almost see the remodeling of the new Tetron Development building. To the left of the new and improved chemistry building was the almost non-existent Tubor memorial. All that was left was a few withered flowers and a few raggedy notes left by friends and loved ones. This supposed tribute had gotten so small that people walked on it without thinking twice. Over time, the memorial had become just another piece of the sidewalk.

I tried desperately to stop looking towards the area where Catherine and I met, but my eyes immediately gravitated to it. The wind picked up and rushed through my jacket and forced it to flap in the wind. I had to get out of this area. This part of campus always did something to me, the stretch of land from the Student Center to the old chemistry building, made me feel like a complete screw-up. Why did Megan have to email me? That night back at the beginning of school felt so long ago. I wished it could stay there, but it is back to the forefront of my mind. She forced it back. There were so many times that I could have contacted her, but I never did, because I felt it would do no good.

I began to remember the time that the priest once told me the story of Job. I sat attentively on his couch that night as he conveyed to me the purpose of faith. God breaking a man down to his bare core to test his faith? What a frail God we pray to. The priest also told me of Sodom and Gomorrah and of the first biblical murderer, Cain. The stories had morals, and the priest thought I would take something away from them. All it did was reassure me that we have not evolved one bit. We were the same jealous and insolent creatures we have been since Adam and Eve, or the Big Bang, or whatever you believe in. God will always test us and in some eyes we will succeed and in others we will fail. I don't know what the priest was thinking when he wasted his time by telling me these parables. They did make me feel validated, but I suppose at times he did have to make attempts at his priestly duties.

Who knew where the priest would end up? I didn't even know if I would ever speak to him again. Megan I would prefer not to, but with the priest I hoped that our paths would cross again. I'd get him to preside over mine and Catherine's shotgun wedding. This thought made me cheerful. I remained outside the computer building, unable to move because of how this area was affecting me. I enjoyed feeling something. I enjoyed being bothered no matter how trivial it might be.

During our last conversation, the priest told me that my outlook was justified. I think he was wrong about that. He had it right all along. Maybe the world isn't perfect, but there has to be ways to just cope. I would be lying to myself if I thought I could change society, or even just change this campus. There has to be a way to just be happy. I didn't want to be miserable or alone anymore.

I couldn't take it anymore! I ran to the payphone and threw a quarter down the vertical slot. I eagerly awaited a dial tone, for the operator to give me permission to make my phone call. I dialed the number that I hadn't dialed in awhile, yet it still seemed so routine to me. Ring, ring, ring, ring, ring, ring…nothing. No answer; only a stupid answering machine. Her soft voice directed people to leave a message. I wanted to speak directly to her, not just to her recorded voice. I wished I could just start over with Catherine, I wished I could feel her head thrust into my shoulder as we tried to walk our separate ways. I wished it could all happen again.

I had to get up, I couldn't stand this area of campus any longer. I had to go somewhere or do something. It was beginning to sicken me, so I headed back towards my dorm room, past the area where Catherine and I had met. I placed my head down and my eyes fixated on the concrete that raced past my eyes as I walked forward. I journeyed up over the stairs and across the walkway between two buildings, my normal route home. I thought about everything that had occurred over the past two semesters, an activity I tended to do often.

Lindsay, the priest, Megan, Alyssa, the cyclist, Randy Tubor, Adam, my roommates, the floating meadow, Jon, and Catherine all burned holes in my mind. Every event replayed itself in my head, and I could feel myself in those situations once again. I could picture the blind date in September, conversations with the priest, swinging the door open to see Megan, the gun smoke filling the campus ending the life of Randy Tubor, my vivid dream, strangling Jon with my bare hands, and making love to Catherine in her room. I remembered how my school sold out to make money, I thought of when a cyclist ran me over, I remembered snorting coke and letting it fly up my nostril, and I remembered just letting go and giving in to it all. Cigarettes, coffee, cocaine, sex, church, and school; I remembered it all. Haunting, beautiful, lonely, ugly, and deranged; my perception of the past year included all of these words.

I continued to walk at a ridiculously fast rate. I walked past nothing because my head was down, and I could see absolutely nothing. I walked over the catwalk without thinking. Suddenly, a head crashed into my shoulder, causing me and the other party to fall back on the concrete and the rocky ground. Her bag fell to the ground, and she scrambled, hoping nobody had seen our carelessness. We fell hard and fast and neither of us saw the other one coming. I looked up and a glimmer appeared in both of our eyes. To this day, I still believe that we would never fall in love if we didn't sometimes walk with our heads down.

Printed in the United States
111513LV00001B/222/P

9 781434 352422